SILENT TRAIL

(A Sheila Stone Suspense Thriller—Book Two)

BLAKE PIERCE

Blake Pierce

Blake Pierce is the USA Today bestselling author of the RILEY PAGE mystery series, which includes seventeen books. Blake Pierce is also the author of the MACKENZIE WHITE mystery series, comprising fourteen books; of the AVERY BLACK mystery series, comprising six books; of the KERI LOCKE mystery series, comprising five books; of the MAKING OF RILEY PAIGE mystery series, comprising six books; of the KATE WISE mystery series, comprising seven books; of the CHLOE FINE psychological suspense mystery, comprising six books; of the JESSIE HUNT psychological suspense thriller series, comprising thirty-five books (and counting); of the AU PAIR psychological suspense thriller series, comprising three books; of the ZOE PRIME mystery series, comprising six books; of the ADELE SHARP mystery series, comprising sixteen books, of the EUROPEAN VOYAGE cozy mystery series, comprising six books; of the LAURA FROST FBI suspense thriller, comprising eleven books; of the ELLA DARK FBI suspense thriller, comprising twenty-one books (and counting); of the A YEAR IN EUROPE cozy mystery series, comprising nine books, of the AVA GOLD mystery series, comprising six books; of the RACHEL GIFT mystery series, comprising thirteen books (and counting); of the VALERIE LAW mystery series, comprising nine books; of the PAIGE KING mystery series, comprising eight books; of the MAY MOORE mystery series, comprising eleven books; of the CORA SHIELDS mystery series, comprising eight books; of the NICKY LYONS mystery series, comprising eight books, of the CAMI LARK mystery series, comprising ten books; of the AMBER YOUNG mystery series, comprising seven books (and counting); of the DAISY FORTUNE mystery series, comprising five books; of the FIONA RED mystery series, comprising eleven books (and counting); of the FAITH BOLD mystery series, comprising eleven books (and counting); of the JULIETTE HART mystery series, comprising five books (and counting); of the MORGAN CROSS mystery series, comprising nine books (and counting); of the FINN WRIGHT mystery series, comprising five books (and counting); of the new SHEILA STONE suspense thriller series, comprising five books (and counting); and of the new RACHEL BLACKWOOD suspense thriller series, comprising five books (and counting).

An avid reader and lifelong fan of the mystery and thriller genres,

Blake loves to hear from you, so please feel free to visit www.blakepierceauthor.com to learn more and stay in touch.

ISBN: 978-1-0943-8363-7

BOOKS BY BLAKE PIERCE

RACHEL BLACKWOOD SUSPENSE THRILLER
NOT THIS WAY (Book #1)
NOT THIS TIME (Book #2)
NOT THIS CLOSE (Book #3)
NOT THIS ROAD (Book #4)
NOT THIS LATE (Book #5)

SHEILA STONE SUSPENSE THRILLER
SILENT GIRL (Book #1)
SILENT TRAIL (Book #2)
SILENT NIGHT (Book #3)
SILENT HOUSE (Book #4)
SILENT SCREAM (Book #5)

FINN WRIGHT MYSTERY SERIES
WHEN YOU'RE MINE (Book #1)
WHEN YOU'RE SAFE (Book #2)
WHEN YOU'RE CLOSE (Book #3)
WHEN YOU'RE SLEEPING (Book #4)
WHEN YOU'RE SANE (Book #5)

MORGAN CROSS MYSTERY SERIES
FOR YOU (Book #1)
FOR RAGE (Book #2)
FOR LUST (Book #3)
FOR WRATH (Book #4)
FOREVER (Book #5)
FOR US (Book #6)
FOR NOW (Book #7)
FOR ONCE (Book #8)
FOR ETERNITY (Book #9)

JULIETTE HART MYSTERY SERIES
NOTHING TO FEAR (Book #1)
NOTHING THERE (Book #2)

NOTHING WATCHING (Book #3)
NOTHING HIDING (Book #4)
NOTHING LEFT (Book #5)

FAITH BOLD MYSTERY SERIES
SO LONG (Book #1)
SO COLD (Book #2)
SO SCARED (Book #3)
SO NORMAL (Book #4)
SO FAR GONE (Book #5)
SO LOST (Book #6)
SO ALONE (Book #7)
SO FORGOTTEN (Book #8)
SO INSANE (Book #9)
SO SMITTEN (Book #10)
SO SIMPLE (Book #11)

FIONA RED MYSTERY SERIES
LET HER GO (Book #1)
LET HER BE (Book #2)
LET HER HOPE (Book #3)
LET HER WISH (Book #4)
LET HER LIVE (Book #5)
LET HER RUN (Book #6)
LET HER HIDE (Book #7)
LET HER BELIEVE (Book #8)
LET HER FORGET (Book #9)
LET HER TRY (Book #10)
LET HER PLAY (Book #11)

DAISY FORTUNE MYSTERY SERIES
NEED YOU (Book #1)
CLAIM YOU (Book #2)
CRAVE YOU (Book #3)
CHOOSE YOU (Book #4)
CHASE YOU (Book #5)

AMBER YOUNG MYSTERY SERIES
ABSENT PITY (Book #1)
ABSENT REMORSE (Book #2)

ABSENT FEELING (Book #3)
ABSENT MERCY (Book #4)
ABSENT REASON (Book #5)
ABSENT SANITY (Book #6)
ABSENT LIFE (Book #7)

CAMI LARK MYSTERY SERIES
JUST ME (Book #1)
JUST OUTSIDE (Book #2)
JUST RIGHT (Book #3)
JUST FORGET (Book #4)
JUST ONCE (Book #5)
JUST HIDE (Book #6)
JUST NOW (Book #7)
JUST HOPE (Book #8)
JUST LEAVE (Book #9)
JUST TONIGHT (Book #10)

NICKY LYONS MYSTERY SERIES
ALL MINE (Book #1)
ALL HIS (Book #2)
ALL HE SEES (Book #3)
ALL ALONE (Book #4)
ALL FOR ONE (Book #5)
ALL HE TAKES (Book #6)
ALL FOR ME (Book #7)
ALL IN (Book #8)

CORA SHIELDS MYSTERY SERIES
UNDONE (Book #1)
UNWANTED (Book #2)
UNHINGED (Book #3)
UNSAID (Book #4)
UNGLUED (Book #5)
UNSTABLE (Book #6)
UNKNOWN (Book #7)
UNAWARE (Book #8)

MAY MOORE SUSPENSE THRILLER
NEVER RUN (Book #1)

NEVER TELL (Book #2)
NEVER LIVE (Book #3)
NEVER HIDE (Book #4)
NEVER FORGIVE (Book #5)
NEVER AGAIN (Book #6)
NEVER LOOK BACK (Book #7)
NEVER FORGET (Book #8)
NEVER LET GO (Book #9)
NEVER PRETEND (Book #10)
NEVER HESITATE (Book #11)

PAIGE KING MYSTERY SERIES
THE GIRL HE PINED (Book #1)
THE GIRL HE CHOSE (Book #2)
THE GIRL HE TOOK (Book #3)
THE GIRL HE WISHED (Book #4)
THE GIRL HE CROWNED (Book #5)
THE GIRL HE WATCHED (Book #6)
THE GIRL HE WANTED (Book #7)
THE GIRL HE CLAIMED (Book #8)

VALERIE LAW MYSTERY SERIES
NO MERCY (Book #1)
NO PITY (Book #2)
NO FEAR (Book #3)
NO SLEEP (Book #4)
NO QUARTER (Book #5)
NO CHANCE (Book #6)
NO REFUGE (Book #7)
NO GRACE (Book #8)
NO ESCAPE (Book #9)

RACHEL GIFT MYSTERY SERIES
HER LAST WISH (Book #1)
HER LAST CHANCE (Book #2)
HER LAST HOPE (Book #3)
HER LAST FEAR (Book #4)
HER LAST CHOICE (Book #5)
HER LAST BREATH (Book #6)
HER LAST MISTAKE (Book #7)

HER LAST DESIRE (Book #8)
HER LAST REGRET (Book #9)
HER LAST HOUR (Book #10)
HER LAST SHOT (Book #11)
HER LAST PRAYER (Book #12)
HER LAST LIE (Book #13)

AVA GOLD MYSTERY SERIES
CITY OF PREY (Book #1)
CITY OF FEAR (Book #2)
CITY OF BONES (Book #3)
CITY OF GHOSTS (Book #4)
CITY OF DEATH (Book #5)
CITY OF VICE (Book #6)

A YEAR IN EUROPE
A MURDER IN PARIS (Book #1)
DEATH IN FLORENCE (Book #2)
VENGEANCE IN VIENNA (Book #3)
A FATALITY IN SPAIN (Book #4)

ELLA DARK FBI SUSPENSE THRILLER
GIRL, ALONE (Book #1)
GIRL, TAKEN (Book #2)
GIRL, HUNTED (Book #3)
GIRL, SILENCED (Book #4)
GIRL, VANISHED (Book 5)
GIRL ERASED (Book #6)
GIRL, FORSAKEN (Book #7)
GIRL, TRAPPED (Book #8)
GIRL, EXPENDABLE (Book #9)
GIRL, ESCAPED (Book #10)
GIRL, HIS (Book #11)
GIRL, LURED (Book #12)
GIRL, MISSING (Book #13)
GIRL, UNKNOWN (Book #14)
GIRL, DECEIVED (Book #15)
GIRL, FORLORN (Book #16)
GIRL, REMADE (Book #17)
GIRL, BETRAYED (Book #18)

GIRL, BOUND (Book #19)
GIRL, REFORMED (Book #20)
GIRL, REBORN (Book #21)

LAURA FROST FBI SUSPENSE THRILLER
ALREADY GONE (Book #1)
ALREADY SEEN (Book #2)
ALREADY TRAPPED (Book #3)
ALREADY MISSING (Book #4)
ALREADY DEAD (Book #5)
ALREADY TAKEN (Book #6)
ALREADY CHOSEN (Book #7)
ALREADY LOST (Book #8)
ALREADY HIS (Book #9)
ALREADY LURED (Book #10)
ALREADY COLD (Book #11)

EUROPEAN VOYAGE COZY MYSTERY SERIES
MURDER (AND BAKLAVA) (Book #1)
DEATH (AND APPLE STRUDEL) (Book #2)
CRIME (AND LAGER) (Book #3)
MISFORTUNE (AND GOUDA) (Book #4)
CALAMITY (AND A DANISH) (Book #5)
MAYHEM (AND HERRING) (Book #6)

ADELE SHARP MYSTERY SERIES
LEFT TO DIE (Book #1)
LEFT TO RUN (Book #2)
LEFT TO HIDE (Book #3)
LEFT TO KILL (Book #4)
LEFT TO MURDER (Book #5)
LEFT TO ENVY (Book #6)
LEFT TO LAPSE (Book #7)
LEFT TO VANISH (Book #8)
LEFT TO HUNT (Book #9)
LEFT TO FEAR (Book #10)
LEFT TO PREY (Book #11)
LEFT TO LURE (Book #12)
LEFT TO CRAVE (Book #13)
LEFT TO LOATHE (Book #14)

LEFT TO HARM (Book #15)
LEFT TO RUIN (Book #16)

THE AU PAIR SERIES
ALMOST GONE (Book#1)
ALMOST LOST (Book #2)
ALMOST DEAD (Book #3)

ZOE PRIME MYSTERY SERIES
FACE OF DEATH (Book#1)
FACE OF MURDER (Book #2)
FACE OF FEAR (Book #3)
FACE OF MADNESS (Book #4)
FACE OF FURY (Book #5)
FACE OF DARKNESS (Book #6)

A JESSIE HUNT PSYCHOLOGICAL SUSPENSE SERIES
THE PERFECT WIFE (Book #1)
THE PERFECT BLOCK (Book #2)
THE PERFECT HOUSE (Book #3)
THE PERFECT SMILE (Book #4)
THE PERFECT LIE (Book #5)
THE PERFECT LOOK (Book #6)
THE PERFECT AFFAIR (Book #7)
THE PERFECT ALIBI (Book #8)
THE PERFECT NEIGHBOR (Book #9)
THE PERFECT DISGUISE (Book #10)
THE PERFECT SECRET (Book #11)
THE PERFECT FAÇADE (Book #12)
THE PERFECT IMPRESSION (Book #13)
THE PERFECT DECEIT (Book #14)
THE PERFECT MISTRESS (Book #15)
THE PERFECT IMAGE (Book #16)
THE PERFECT VEIL (Book #17)
THE PERFECT INDISCRETION (Book #18)
THE PERFECT RUMOR (Book #19)
THE PERFECT COUPLE (Book #20)
THE PERFECT MURDER (Book #21)
THE PERFECT HUSBAND (Book #22)
THE PERFECT SCANDAL (Book #23)

THE PERFECT MASK (Book #24)
THE PERFECT RUSE (Book #25)
THE PERFECT VENEER (Book #26)
THE PERFECT PEOPLE (Book #27)
THE PERFECT WITNESS (Book #28)
THE PERFECT APPEARANCE (Book #29)
THE PERFECT TRAP (Book #30)
THE PERFECT EXPRESSION (Book #31)
THE PERFECT ACCOMPLICE (Book #32)
THE PERFECT SHOW (Book #33)
THE PERFECT POISE (Book #34)
THE PERFECT CROWD (Book #35)

CHLOE FINE PSYCHOLOGICAL SUSPENSE SERIES
NEXT DOOR (Book #1)
A NEIGHBOR'S LIE (Book #2)
CUL DE SAC (Book #3)
SILENT NEIGHBOR (Book #4)
HOMECOMING (Book #5)
TINTED WINDOWS (Book #6)

KATE WISE MYSTERY SERIES
IF SHE KNEW (Book #1)
IF SHE SAW (Book #2)
IF SHE RAN (Book #3)
IF SHE HID (Book #4)
IF SHE FLED (Book #5)
IF SHE FEARED (Book #6)
IF SHE HEARD (Book #7)

THE MAKING OF RILEY PAIGE SERIES
WATCHING (Book #1)
WAITING (Book #2)
LURING (Book #3)
TAKING (Book #4)
STALKING (Book #5)
KILLING (Book #6)

RILEY PAIGE MYSTERY SERIES
ONCE GONE (Book #1)

ONCE TAKEN (Book #2)
ONCE CRAVED (Book #3)
ONCE LURED (Book #4)
ONCE HUNTED (Book #5)
ONCE PINED (Book #6)
ONCE FORSAKEN (Book #7)
ONCE COLD (Book #8)
ONCE STALKED (Book #9)
ONCE LOST (Book #10)
ONCE BURIED (Book #11)
ONCE BOUND (Book #12)
ONCE TRAPPED (Book #13)
ONCE DORMANT (Book #14)
ONCE SHUNNED (Book #15)
ONCE MISSED (Book #16)
ONCE CHOSEN (Book #17)

MACKENZIE WHITE MYSTERY SERIES
BEFORE HE KILLS (Book #1)
BEFORE HE SEES (Book #2)
BEFORE HE COVETS (Book #3)
BEFORE HE TAKES (Book #4)
BEFORE HE NEEDS (Book #5)
BEFORE HE FEELS (Book #6)
BEFORE HE SINS (Book #7)
BEFORE HE HUNTS (Book #8)
BEFORE HE PREYS (Book #9)
BEFORE HE LONGS (Book #10)
BEFORE HE LAPSES (Book #11)
BEFORE HE ENVIES (Book #12)
BEFORE HE STALKS (Book #13)
BEFORE HE HARMS (Book #14)

AVERY BLACK MYSTERY SERIES
CAUSE TO KILL (Book #1)
CAUSE TO RUN (Book #2)
CAUSE TO HIDE (Book #3)
CAUSE TO FEAR (Book #4)
CAUSE TO SAVE (Book #5)
CAUSE TO DREAD (Book #6)

KERI LOCKE MYSTERY SERIES

A TRACE OF DEATH (Book #1)
A TRACE OF MURDER (Book #2)
A TRACE OF VICE (Book #3)
A TRACE OF CRIME (Book #4)
A TRACE OF HOPE (Book #5)

PROLOGUE

Rita tugged at the door handle, but it remained stubbornly locked. Her breath misted in the chilly, pre-dawn air as she sighed in frustration.

"Mrs. Hayfield was supposed to be here by now," she muttered under her breath. She pulled out her phone, its battery indicator blinking ominously low, and quickly typed out a message to her teacher, hoping for a prompt response.

As she leaned against the door, she couldn't help but feel a pang of disappointment—her first event at college, and she was already off to a rocky start.

Surrounded by the hushed beauty of the Utah landscape, Coldwater Community College seemed like an oasis of learning and growth. Rita had fallen in love with the picturesque campus on her first visit, drawn to its serene atmosphere and promise of academic opportunities. Now, standing alone in the dim morning light, she felt a mixture of anticipation and anxiety churning within her.

The silence was broken only by the distant chirping of birds and the rustling of autumn leaves underfoot as squirrels darted among the trees. Rita glanced around, taking in the majestic snow-capped mountains in the distance and the neatly manicured lawns that rolled out between the red-brick buildings. It was still early in the semester, and most of the students weren't due to arrive for another hour or so. But Rita had hoped to make a good impression on her teachers and peers alike by showing up early to help set up for the event.

Where's Claire, anyway? she wondered. *We were supposed to meet up here. If she's skipping class again, I'm going to strangle her. I don't care how bad her hangover is.*

It hadn't taken long for Rita to realize that her ambitions didn't always match up with those of her new friends. While most of them were at Coldwater Community College for the party scene, Rita had come to learn. As a freshman pursuing a degree in forensic psychology, she was fascinated by the human mind and its darker corners. She hoped one day to work alongside law enforcement, helping to catch criminals and bring justice to victims. Her friends couldn't understand why she'd rather spend her weekends buried in books than dancing the night away, but to Rita, it was simple: she wanted to make something of herself.

The event she and Claire were supposed to set up was an icebreaker for new students, organized by the college's Psychology Club. It would be a chance for fellow psych majors to mingle and form connections that could last throughout their academic careers—or so the club president had said in one of their meetings. Rita had volunteered to help set up the decorations, eager to prove her dedication to the group and make a good first impression on her peers.

Her thoughts were interrupted when a shadow fell over her. Startled, Rita turned around to find Claire standing behind her, a playful smirk on her lips.

"Still waiting for Mrs. Hayfield?" Claire asked, her voice dripping with amusement. "You're at the wrong door, genius. The entrance we need is just around the corner."

"Really?" Rita frowned, feeling foolish. "Thanks," she mumbled, slipping her phone back into her pocket as she followed Claire.

As they walked toward the correct door, Rita couldn't help but study Claire. The older girl moved with an easy grace, her long legs carrying her effortlessly across the campus grounds. Dressed in a stylish outfit and matching sneakers, she looked every bit the part of a college athlete—which, of course, she was. A star on the volleyball team, Claire seemed to have it all: athleticism, popularity, and an effortless confidence that drew people to her like moths to a flame.

Rita tried to suppress a twinge of envy as she trailed behind Claire, her own academic ambitions momentarily overshadowed by the realization that she lacked the social ease that came so naturally to her companion. While Rita was proud of her commitment to her studies, she sometimes wished she could let loose and enjoy the more carefree side of college life—just like Claire seemed to do without even trying.

"Trust me," Claire said, flashing Rita a dazzling smile as they reached the entrance, "you'll know this place like the back of your hand by the end of semester. Then you can come and go as you please, and no one will be the wiser." She winked.

The heavy doors swung open, revealing the spacious interior of Coldwater Community College's Hempstead Building. High ceilings and wide corridors provided an airy atmosphere, while the polished floors reflected the soft glow of overhead lights. The walls were adorned with colorful banners and posters advertising various clubs and events, adding to the vibrant energy of the campus.

"By the way," Claire continued, her voice dropping conspiratorially as they walked deeper into the building, "did I tell you about the prank we pulled on Professor Jenkins last week? We snuck into his office after hours and filled it with balloons. It took him ages to sort it out the next morning."

Rita chuckled, despite herself. The idea of their stern, bespectacled professor wading through a sea of balloons was undeniably amusing.

"You should join us next time," Claire said. "Get in on the action."

"Sounds like fun," Rita admitted, "but I really need to focus on my studies right now. I don't want to fall behind in my classes."

Claire rolled her eyes playfully, nudging Rita with her elbow. "Come on, lighten up a little! College is about more than just reading books. You've got to have some fun every now and then, too."

They finally arrived at the conference room where the Psychology Club event was to be held. The room was spacious, with large windows lining one wall and letting in the soft morning light. Rows of round tables stood bare, awaiting their adornments.

"Alright," Claire said as she clapped her hands together, her eyes sparkling with excitement. "Let's get this party started."

Together, they began unpacking boxes filled with tablecloths, candles, and various other decorations. As Rita unfolded a deep blue tablecloth, she couldn't help but marvel at the intricate gold patterns embroidered along the edges. She glanced over at Claire, who was already setting up elaborate centerpieces with practiced ease.

"Hey, these look great!" Rita said, trying to match her friend's enthusiasm. "I can't wait to see everything when it's finished."

Claire grinned, her confidence radiating through the room. "Trust me; it's going to be amazing."

As Rita continued to work, she focused on the task at hand, laying out each tablecloth carefully and adjusting the centerpieces just so. But she couldn't shake the feeling that something was missing. It wasn't until Claire suddenly cursed under her breath that Rita realized she wasn't alone in her concerns.

"Everything okay?" Rita asked, furrowing her brow.

"No," Claire replied, her frustration evident. "We're missing the masquerade masks—we need them for one of the games. They must still be in the supply closet."

"Okay," Rita said, straightening her shoulders. "Just tell me where the closet is, and I'll go grab them."

"Are you sure?" Claire hesitated, biting her lip. "It's kind of a long walk from here."

"Of course," Rita said, eager to prove herself useful. "I don't mind at all."

"Okay, so you're going to want to go down this hallway and take the first right," Claire told Rita, gesturing in the direction of a long corridor lined with brightly colored doors. "Follow that until you reach the main atrium. Once you're there, make a left and go past the library. Then, take another left at the end of that hallway. The supply closet is just a few doors down on your right."

"Okay," Rita said slowly, trying to commit the directions to memory.

"Got all that?" There was a note of doubt in Claire's voice.

"I think so. If not, I'll come back."

"Or you'll get lost and never be heard from again."

Rita smiled, though the words sent shivers down her spine. "The college isn't *that* big."

"You'd be surprised. Now get going!" Claire waved a hand at her. "We really need those decorations before students start arriving."

Rita nodded and set off at a brisk pace, repeating Claire's directions to herself under her breath.

The early morning sun streamed through the large windows, casting warm golden light across the polished floors and freshly painted walls. The college was quiet at this hour, most of its inhabitants still tucked away in bed or just beginning their day. The silence felt both comforting and eerie, as though Rita were exploring an abandoned world.

As she hurried through the campus, Rita marveled at the rows of classrooms and lecture halls, each one representing a new opportunity for growth and learning. She imagined herself sitting in those rooms, absorbing knowledge and working tirelessly toward her goals.

When Rita had followed most of Claire's directions, she reached a dark hallway. The contrast between the brightly lit corridors she'd just left and the gloom that enveloped this stretch of the building was striking, and she felt strangely uneasy.

Had someone forgotten to turn the overhead lights on?

Her fingers brushed along the cold, smooth surface of the wall, searching for a light switch. The darkness seemed to press in on her from all sides as she fumbled blindly. Her heart rate kicked up a notch, and she could feel the dampness of sweat gathering at the nape of her neck.

"Come on," she muttered to herself, frustration mounting. She pulled out her phone, hoping it would provide enough light to help her find the switch or light the hallway ahead of her. The screen, however, gave no more than a faint flicker before giving up the ghost completely—her battery had finally run out. With a resigned sigh, Rita decided she would have to brave the dark hallway without the aid of artificial light.

As she stepped further into the shadows, her thoughts turned to the stories she'd heard whispered around campus—tales of sinister figures lurking in the darkness, waiting to prey on unsuspecting students. She shuddered involuntarily but pushed the fear aside. It was ridiculous to be scared of the dark, especially when there was important work to be done.

With her heart thudding in her ears, Rita quickened her pace, eager to reach the other side of the hallway. The clap of her footsteps provided her with a strange sense of comfort amidst the oppressive gloom.

Finally, she reached the door of the supply closet. Fumbling for the handle, she swung it open to reveal a small, cramped space packed with boxes and miscellaneous supplies. The overhead light flickered to life with an almost imperceptible hum, casting eerie shadows across the walls.

Rita breathed a sigh of relief, grateful for the illumination. She scanned the shelves, her eyes darting over stacks of paper, binders, and cleaning supplies before landing on what she'd been searching for—the box of masquerade masks. Grabbing the box, she took one last look around the cluttered closet before stepping back into the dark hallway, a newfound determination propelling her forward.

She trotted through the darkness, all too aware of how long she'd taken to find the closet. Then she picked up the pace even more, hurrying through the building, her mind doing mental gymnastics as she tried to plot her way.

Somehow, she managed to find the conference room again. She burst through the doorway, her breaths coming in heavy pants as she clutched the box. The atmosphere had shifted dramatically since she had left—students now filled the once-empty space, their excited chatter mingling with the rustle of fabric and the scrape of chairs as they prepared for the event.

Claire stood on a stepladder near the front of the room, expertly looping streamers around the ceiling beams. Her lithe form was silhouetted against the morning light filtering through the windows, which bathed her long, dark hair in a golden halo. Rita couldn't help but admire Claire's effortless grace, even in such a mundane task.

"Finally!" Claire called down, hopping off the ladder to face Rita. "What took you so long?"

"Sorry," Rita mumbled, feeling her cheeks heat up. "It was a long way."

"Typical freshman," Claire teased, but her tone was gentle. She gestured toward the far corner of the room. "Start hanging those banners over there. We've got to get this place looking festive before everyone arrives."

As Rita dutifully began her task, she felt Claire's eyes on her. Glancing up, she saw her friend frown, her gaze fixed on the floor. "What's wrong?" Rita asked, concern edging into her voice.

"Your footprints," Claire said, pointing at the carpet beneath Rita's sneakers. A trail of red stains marred the otherwise pristine surface.

Puzzled, Rita stared at the stains, wondering how she could have possibly tracked in something so vibrant. As the implications of the crimson marks began to dawn on her, a sick feeling settled in the pit of her stomach.

"What in the world did you step in?" Claire asked.

Rita shrugged helplessly. "I have no idea."

Without a word, the two friends began retracing the footsteps. The trail of red led them back to the dark hallway, which now seemed even more menacing than before. As Claire illuminated the space with her phone's flashlight, shadows danced ominously along the walls. A row of lockers lined one side of the corridor, their metal surfaces gleaming in the artificial light.

As they drew nearer, Rita noticed a thick, viscous liquid dripping from the bottom of one of the lockers—the same color as the stains on the carpet. Now, there could be no question about what it was.

Blood.

Rita's heart pounded in her chest, each beat echoing in her ears as she stepped closer to the locker, drawn by a morbid curiosity.

"This can't be happening," Claire said, though her voice trembled with fear and her face had paled considerably.

With trembling hands, Rita grasped the cold handle of the locker. Then she paused as a new idea occurred to her. She relaxed her shoulders, breathing more easily. Claire was right—this couldn't be happening.

Which meant there was only one explanation.

"Hardy-har-har," she said, rolling her eyes at Claire. "You really had me going there for a minute, you know. What was the plan? I open the door, all terrified, and a Halloween skeleton falls on me or something? Was that the idea?"

Claire just stared at her, wide-eyed. Oh, she knew how to act when she wanted to. Her acting was so impressive, in fact, that Rita felt a flicker of doubt. But that was ridiculous. There was no way this could be real.

Suddenly, she had to know the truth for certain. Holding her breath, putting on a tight smile to show she was not about to be the butt of the joke, she hauled the locker open.

It's just a prank, just a prank, she told herself. *It's just a—*

And then the body fell on her.

CHAPTER ONE

Sheila tapped her fingers on the steering wheel of the van, the rhythmic beat punctuating the silence of the early morning. She stared at the door of her sister's house as if willing it to open with the sheer force of her gaze.

"Come on, Natalie," she muttered under her breath, glancing at the time displayed on her dashboard. Seven in the morning.

The house itself was modest and well-maintained, its pale yellow siding complementing the surrounding flower beds filled with late-blooming perennials. The neighborhood was picturesque, the kind of place where kids played outside until dusk, and neighbors exchanged pleasantries over white picket fences. But Sheila couldn't help staring at the recently-installed ramp leading up to the front door, a stark reminder of how much had changed in such a short period of time.

Her heart thudded in her chest, a feeling of unease settling over her like a heavy fog. She had been driving Natalie to work for the past month, but the sight of her sister navigating life with limited mobility still left her disconcerted.

A bead of sweat trickled down Sheila's temple as she tried to shake off the guilt that gnawed at her insides. If only she had done things differently during their investigation together – hadn't gotten herself caught by a psychotic killer and forced Natalie to confront him at the side of the road in the middle of nowhere, with no backup in sight – maybe then, Natalie wouldn't be in this situation. But the question that haunted her the most was whether Natalie harbored any resentment toward her for it.

Does she blame me? She hasn't said anything to that effect, but still, I can't help feeling like she's treating me differently now. She can be so...aloof.

The creak of the front door yanked her out of her thoughts. There was Natalie, dressed in her sheriff's uniform, expertly maneuvering her wheelchair down the ramp. Her jaw clenched as she struggled to close the door behind her, her fingers grasping for the handle while she balanced on one wheel.

"Hey, let me help you with that," Sheila said, stepping out of the van and hurrying to assist her sister.

Natalie flashed a tight smile, her eyes not quite meeting Sheila's. "No, I'm fine, really. I've got it." With a final tug, she managed to shut the door and roll away from the house, her movements more labored than before.

"Okay, if you're sure..." Sheila trailed off, uncertainty lingering in her voice. She couldn't tell if the tension she sensed in Natalie was genuine or just a figment of her own guilty conscience.

Sheila averted her eyes as Natalie approached, pretending to be engrossed in the vibrant colors of the late summer foliage lining the quiet street. In reality, she couldn't stand to see her sister struggling with the wheelchair, each push of the wheels a reminder of the bullet that had grazed her spinal column.

A bullet that, if Natalie hadn't pushed Sheila out of the way, might have struck Sheila instead.

As Natalie reached the van, Sheila opened the side door, revealing a chair lift installed on the floor of the van. Sheila pressed a button, causing the lift to slowly emerge from the van before sinking to the ground, and then watched as Natalie parked her chair on the lift. A moment later, Natalie was rising in the air, her jaw clenched as she couldn't bear how complicated getting into a vehicle had become for her.

Returning to the driver's seat, Sheila started the engine and pulled out of the driveway, the tires crunching over gravel as the van eased onto the quiet street. The neighborhood was still waking up, a sleepy tableau of modest houses nestled beneath the towering Wasatch Range that framed the eastern horizon. As they drove, the sun crept ever higher, casting long shadows across the landscape and bathing everything in a warm, honeyed light.

Despite the beauty, Sheila found herself drumming her fingers nervously on the steering wheel. The silence between her and Natalie felt thick, suffocating—a vast canyon where easy conversation had once flowed effortlessly. Desperate to fill the void, she cast about for any topic that might bridge the gap.

"So," she said, trying to start a conversation, "have you spoken with Dad lately?" She stole a glance at Natalie in the rearview mirror.

"Not much," Natalie said, staring out the window. "I'm busy, he's busy—it's not like when I was a kid and we were living in the same house, you know?"

Sheila nodded. "I get it. It takes so much more effort now to plan things. It doesn't just happen incidentally—you have to plan it, look at your schedule, find something that works for both sides. Life was so much simpler when we were kids, wasn't it?"

Natalie murmured noncommittally as she studied her phone. Studying Natalie in the mirror again, Sheila found herself yearning for the closeness they once shared. Each attempt to reach out, however, felt like grasping at smoke.

"Look at those mountains," she said, gesturing toward the jagged peaks that loomed like ancient sentinels in the distance. "Always makes me feel so small, y'know?"

Natalie nodded, her gaze following Sheila's. "Yeah, I've always loved the view."

Encouraged by her sister's response, Sheila pressed on, trying to find a way to relate with Natalie. "I know what it's like, you know—feeling trapped by your own body. After my head injury, I couldn't train like I used to. It felt like my whole world had been turned upside down."

She hesitated, then added softly, "But, in a way, I think it brought us closer. If I hadn't gotten hurt, I wouldn't be here now, helping you with cases and...well, spending time together."

Natalie's brow furrowed, her lips pressing into a thin line as Sheila's words hung heavy in the air between them. For a moment, silence reigned once more, broken only by the hum of the engine and the rhythmic thump of the tires against the asphalt below.

Finally, Natalie spoke, her voice tight with restrained emotion. "I appreciate that. I do. But it's not quite the same, is it?"

Sheila swallowed hard, the knot in her throat tightening as she searched for the right words.

Natalie's smile was wistful, tinged with a sadness that made Sheila's chest tighten. "I know you mean well, Sheila. But the truth is, your injury doesn't affect your everyday life like mine does."

The stark honesty in Natalie's words struck a chord within Sheila, forcing her to confront the reality of their situation. A month ago, she had been the one adrift, searching for purpose in the wake of her Olympic dreams shattering due to a head injury that could have proven life-threatening. It was Natalie who had thrown her a lifeline, inviting her to join the investigation and, in doing so, setting her on a new path. Now, as she considered a future in law enforcement, it was her sister who found herself struggling to make sense of the hand fate had dealt her.

As Sheila searched for the right words to respond to Natalie, her sister's phone rang, disrupting the moment.

"This is Natalie," Natalie said, her gaze sliding to the window. She listened for several moments, saying nothing. "Okay. Yes, I understand. We'll be there as soon as we can." She hung up and looked at Sheila. "That was Finn. We need to head to Coldwater Community College ASAP."

"Three-C?" Sheila asked, recalling the nickname many locals had for the college. "What's waiting for you there?"

"A body," Natalie answered, her jaw set and her voice serious. "And judging by the number of times she was stabbed, I'd say it was very personal."

CHAPTER TWO

Sheila gripped the steering wheel as she guided the van into the parking lot of Coldwater Community College, her knuckles whitening with each turn. She could feel the weight of silence pressing against her chest, making it difficult to breathe. Natalie, sitting beside her, stared blankly at the passing scenery, her mind seemingly far away.

Why won't she talk to me? Sheila wondered. *I know she's devastated to be in a wheelchair...but does she blame me for it?*

It was late summer in Utah. The morning sun cast a warm golden glow over the college campus, but its comforting embrace seemed wasted on Sheila. She more than ready to drop Natalie off and get on with her day.

As they drove through the campus, Sheila was struck by how many police cruisers were already on site, their blue and red lights flashing in stark contrast to the morning calm. Clusters of students stood around, exchanging worried glances and whispered speculations. Classes must have been canceled for the day—no surprise, given what had happened.

"I wonder what they're all thinking," Sheila said, breaking the silence. She couldn't bear the quiet any longer, and she hoped that she might draw her sister out now that they had something external to focus on.

Natalie, however, didn't respond, her gaze fixed on the chaotic scene unfolding before them. Sheila sighed, her shoulders sagging under the weight of her sister's continued detachment. All she wanted was to drop Natalie off and escape to the gym, where she could push herself harder than she had since her head injury. Maybe there, amid the grunts of exertion and the dull thud of fists hitting bags, she could find solace from the relentless thoughts of failure that haunted her waking hours.

"Park right here," Natalie finally murmured. "I think I see Finn."

Sheila did so. Then she turned off the engine and got out of the van, walking around the vehicle so she could open Natalie's door for her. Natalie, however, had already opened the door, and there was a faint hum as the lift lowered her wheelchair to the asphalt.

"I'm not entirely helpless," Natalie said, a small smile playing on her lips as though nothing was amiss between them. Sheila forced a smile in return, playing along with the fiction.

As Sheila took a step back toward the driver's side, Deputy Finn Mercer appeared around the building, his stride confident but his expression tense. When he caught sight of them, he hesitated for a moment, his step hitching as he spotting Natalie. It was subtle, but Sheila had a feeling her sister hadn't missed it, either.

He's not quite sure how to behave around her, Sheila thought. *He's not used to taking orders from someone in a wheelchair.*

"There you are," Natalie said, her voice giving no hint that she had noticed his hesitation. "Just in time to show me to the crime scene."

Finn cleared his throat, his eyes shifting to Sheila for a moment before returning to Natalie. "Actually, there's something you should know first," he said. "I just learned there was another murder two days ago at Elbridge College."

"You think they're connected?" Natalie asked.

"Looks like there's a good chance. Both victims were female college students, both of them athletes, and most striking of all, both were found shut in their lockers."

Sheila cursed softly, her stomach twisting at the thought. A shiver ran down her spine as she imagined the horror of finding a teammate like that. She hesitated, her hand on the handle of the van's door, wanting to leave but also curious to hear more.

"Have they been identified yet?" Natalie asked.

Finn nodded. "The victim at Elbridge College was Jane Johnson, a runner on the track team. The victim here at Coldwater College was Kristen Lee, a volleyball player."

Sheila's mind was already racing with questions. What could drive someone to target young, promising athletes like that? And why had their bodies been put in their lockers?

"Cause of death?" Natalie asked, rolling toward Finn.

"Stabbing," Finn answered. "Judging by the number of wounds, I'd say someone was pretty damn angry."

Sheila shifted her weight from one foot to the other, eager to get going. As interesting as this all sounded, she felt a need to have some time to herself. Natalie and Finn were more than capable of handling this investigation without her.

"Good seeing you, Finn," she said, waving to the deputy. "I'm going to hit the gym." She had just climbed into the driver's seat and was about to close the door when Natalie's voice reached her.

"Wait," Natalie said, staring thoughtfully at her through the windshield. "You know, Sheila, we could really use your expertise on this one, given your background in the sports world."

Sheila rose and leaned her forearms on the open door of the van. "I don't know the sports world any better than you do, Nat."

"That's not true. I've been out of the game for a while, but you're fresh from the ring."

Thanks for that reminder, Sheila thought. Only two months had passed since her elimination from Olympic competition, and the defeat was still fresh in her mind.

"Come on," Natalie said softly. "You can go to the gym any day. This is an opportunity to make a real difference, Sheila."

Sheila hesitated, biting her lip as she weighed her options. A part of her yearned for the familiarity and comfort of the gym, where she could lose herself in the rhythm of her kicks and punches. But Natalie was right: She could go to the gym any time she pleased.

It's not about going to the gym. It's about being around Natalie. Do I really want to spend all day with her, questioning whether or not she's being passive-aggressive?

"If not for yourself," Natalie said, "then do it for Finn. It's been a while since he trained anyone, so it would be good for him to have the chance to show you the ropes. You're going to need all the experience you can get if you want to be more than a consultant." She winked.

Sheila's potential future in law enforcement was not a subject they'd discussed much since Natalie's injury. That didn't mean it hadn't been on Sheila's mind, though. Here was a chance to make a real difference, and by the sound of it, she and Natalie would get a little breathing room from each other, too.

"What are you going to do?" she asked, feigning disappointment at the prospect of not working alongside Natalie.

"Working at my own pace instead of slowing you two down," Natalie answered. "But don't worry: We'll be in constant communication. I'll still be very much involved, just from a different angle."

Sheila felt a twinge of guilt at the reminder of Natalie's limitations but knew better than to argue with her stubborn sister. Instead, she nodded, trying to quell the unease that twisted in her gut. She glanced over at Finn, who stood a few feet away, watching their exchange with a hint of curiosity. He offered her a half-smile that Sheila couldn't quite read.

"Okay," Sheila said finally, nodding. "I'll help if I can."

"Great!" Natalie said, brightening. "Finn will look after you. I've got a conference call with the state police and the college president, but I'll catch up with you both later."

With that, she rolled away, the wheels of the wheelchair clicking on the pavement as she headed to the administration building.

"Don't worry," Finn said as Sheila stared after her sister. "She can look after herself."

Sheila nodded, taking Finn's words to heart. She cleared her throat and turned to the deputy. "So," she asked, her voice betraying a hint of uncertainty, "where should we start?"

"At the locker," he said. "Follow me."

CHAPTER THREE

As Sheila followed Finn along Coldwater Community College's eerily quiet corridors, she couldn't help but wonder if Natalie had purposely paired her with Finn in order to keep an eye on her. The thought stung, and she quickly tried to dismiss it, but doubt lingered at the edges of her mind.

The college's interior was modest yet welcoming, with beige walls adorned by student artwork and bulletin boards announcing upcoming events. Despite the late summer warmth outside, the air inside was cool and crisp, carrying the faint scent of chalk and cleaning supplies. It was unnervingly silent, as if the building itself were holding its breath, waiting for something to happen.

"Where is everyone?" Sheila asked, unable to contain her curiosity any longer.

Finn glanced back at her, his expression unreadable. "Most of the students are out on the soccer fields," he replied. "Officers are interviewing them about the incident, trying to determine whether anyone might have seen anything."

As they continued down the hallway, Sheila found her gaze drifting to Finn. He moved with a quiet confidence, his posture straight and his shoulders squared. There was a mysterious air about him that intrigued her. She tried to recall any information Natalie had shared about him, but came up empty. She couldn't help but wonder how he'd adapted to Natalie's injury—whether it had changed their working relationship in any meaningful way.

"Almost there," Finn said, pulling her from her thoughts. He paused in front of a section of lockers, cordoned off by yellow crime scene tape. The morning sunlight filtering through nearby windows illuminated the gruesome scene, casting eerie shadows on the floor.

Sheila's heart quickened as she took in the sight before her. Blood splattered the inside of the open locker, and there was a small pool of it on the linoleum below as well, a chilling reminder of the violence the victim had suffered. A chaotic series of bloody footprints covered the area, along with drag marks where the blood streaked the floor.

Finn's voice broke the silence, shattering her reverie. "Kristen Lee was a junior here," he said. "Played for the volleyball team. A better athlete than a student, by all accounts. She was majoring in biology."

Sheila studied the chaotic scene, trying to make sense of what had happened. "Did the killer leave these footprints?" she asked, pointing.

Finn shook his head. "No, it would've taken time for the blood to pool like this. The killer would've had to stick around long enough for the blood to pool, then accidentally step in it, thus leaving incriminating prints. Not very likely." He paused to look at her. "Plus, one of the girls who found the body admitted to stepping in the blood, so I think it's pretty clear what happened." He winked at her.

Sheila's cheeks flushed with embarrassment. She should have deduced on her own how unlikely it was that the killer could have left the prints, but she was very new to this world of crime-solving, and every misstep served as a reminder of just how much she had to learn.

"Right," she said. "So, we can rule out the footprints as evidence left by the killer."

"Correct," Finn said, his tone neutral.

Wanting to move past her mistake, Sheila decided to change the subject. "Tell me about the two girls who found Lee's body," she said, hoping to gain more insight into the situation.

"Rita Cohen and Claire Hutchinson," Finn began, his voice taking on a hint of authority as he recounted the information. "They opened the locker after Rita accidentally stepped in the blood."

"She stepped in the blood? How did she not see it?"

"The hallway was dark because some of the overhead lights were out—apparently a work order was put in to have the lights replaced, but the electrician hasn't been in yet."

"What happened after they opened the locker?" Sheila asked.

Finn shrugged one shoulder. "They screamed and ran. That's about the short of it, anyway, as far as I know. If you want more details, you'll have to talk to them directly. I'm just telling you what I heard from the officer who responded to the call."

Sheila mulled over the details, trying to piece together the puzzle. As her eyes scanned the crime scene once more, her attention was drawn to the streaks in the blood. It looked as though something had been dragged across the floor.

"Hey, Finn," she said cautiously, her brow furrowed in concentration. "Doesn't it look like the body might have been moved? What else would have caused these marks?"

Finn studied the traces of blood on the ground, his expression thoughtful. "It's possible. But why would someone move the body? The killer obviously wanted her in the locker."

Sheila grew thoughtful, her mind chasing down different possibilities. "Can you tell me where the nearest restroom is? I want to check something."

Finn straightened and looked down the hallway, first one way and then the other. "Let's go find out," he said.

Sheila and Finn walked down the hall, side by side. Before long, they saw a pair of signs, one for the men's restroom and the other for the women's. As Sheila entered the women's restroom, Finn hesitated.

"Come on," Sheila said. "I appreciate your sense of propriety, but this is murder we're talking about."

His eyes were glassy, stoic. Then, with a shrug, he gestured for her to go first.

Sheila pushed open the door to the ladies' restroom, the faint scent of lemon-scented cleaner wafting through the air. The room was pristine, with spotless white tiles reflecting the overhead fluorescent lighting. Three sinks lined one wall, their sleek chrome faucets gleaming under the harsh light.

"So what are we looking for?" Finn asked as he followed her inside, his voice rebounding off the tiled walls.

Sheila's gaze darted from sink to sink, her intuition telling her that the answer she sought lay hidden in this seemingly untouched sanctuary. She approached each faucet in turn, crouching down to study the undersides of the handles. The first two looked clean. As she reached the last sink, however, her heart skipped a beat—there, nearly invisible against the polished metal, were faint smears of dried blood.

"Look at this," she said, pointing out the incriminating evidence to Finn.

He frowned, leaning in for a closer look. "That's definitely blood. What do you think it means?"

Sheila straightened up, her mind racing through possible scenarios. "I think someone tried to move the body and then came in here to wash up," she said slowly, carefully weighing each word.

"The killer, maybe?"

"It's possible…but it's equally possible Rita and Claire came in here to wash up after moving the body. Just because they called in the body doesn't mean they're innocent."

"You think they're lying," Finn said.

Sheila said nothing. Following her instincts, she headed to the trash receptacle in the corner of the room. She pawed through a pile of discarded paper towels before finding what she was looking for.

Pulling it out of the trash, she held the sweatshirt up for Finn to see. It was a woman's sweatshirt.

And, more importantly, there was a large bloodstain on the front and the sleeves.

CHAPTER FOUR

Sheila tried to imitate Finn's stoicism as she approached the classroom where Rita Cohen and Claire Hutchinson were waiting, but she found it difficult to hide how she truly felt. She believed the two girls had tried to move Kristen Lee's body, then lied about it to the police, and she wanted to know why.

She just hoped they wouldn't see the suspicion in her eyes when she met them.

As they entered the room, Sheila took in the scene before her. The classroom was typically used for psychology lectures, as evidenced by the large whiteboard filled with notes about human behavior and the rows of desks facing the front. However, today, it serves as a very different sort of forum for human behavior.

The air hung heavy with tension, and the somber expressions on both Rita's and Claire's faces spoke volumes. They sat at a pair of desks pushed together, their hands clasped tightly in their laps. Behind them stood a man with his arms crossed, looking on with an expression of thinly-veiled impatience.

There was a fourth individual in the room: a slim police officer with nut-brown eyes and a mustache as thin as a whisper. He was speaking to the other man in a low voice, but when he saw Sheila and Finn enter the room, he broke away and approached them.

"Deputy Mercer," he said with a curt nod. "Good to see you again."

"Likewise, Garner," Finn replied, his tone equally reserved. "This is Sheila Stone. She's working with us on this case."

"Nice to meet you, Ms. Stone," Garner said, extending a hand that Sheila shook hesitantly, feeling a bit out of place. It felt strange, working with the police without actually being one of them, almost as if she were an impostor.

"Likewise," she said with a polite nod.

Garner leaned in closer, his voice dropping to a low whisper. "They were pretty shaken up when we first brought them in, but they've calmed down some. You might be able to get more information from them now."

"Thanks for the update," Finn said, exchanging a quick glance with Sheila before they turned their attention to the two girls huddled together at the desk. "Which one is which?"

"The one on the left is Miss Cohen," Garner said. "The one on the right is Miss Hutchinson."

Rita Cohen was petite, with curly brown hair and an almost childlike innocence about her. Her friend, Claire Hutchinson, was taller, with long blonde hair pulled back into a ponytail. There was something haughty about Claire's gaze, as if she were continually assessing where she belonged in the pecking order—and usually judging herself to be higher than those she met.

Claire, Sheila noticed, was wearing a zip-up hoodie, while Rita wore a short-sleeved shirt.

"And the man standing behind them?" Sheila asked.

Garner hesitated just a moment. "That's Roger Hutchinson, Claire's dad. He's...very upset about all this. I've had to tell him twice now why he can't take Claire home just yet."

Sheila nodded, studying the man who was in turn staring back, his gaze imperious.

He sure doesn't look very happy to see us, Sheila thought.

Finn introduced himself and Sheila as they approached the two girls. "You must be Miss Cohen and Miss Hutchinson, is that right?" he asked.

Before either girl could answer, Roger Hutchinson spoke up. "What's she doing here?" he asked gruffly, pointing at Sheila. "She's not police. So what is she, a reporter?"

Sheila felt a surge of annoyance but kept her emotions in check. He was undoubtedly referring to the fact that she, unlike the other two officers, was not in uniform.

"Sheila is a consultant working with our department, not an official officer," Finn said.

"Consultant?" Mr. Hutchinson snorted derisively. "What, does the sheriff's department not have the funding to train real police officers?"

Sheila felt her cheeks redden and her fists clench at her sides, but she forced herself to remain calm. She knew her background as a kickboxer and her sister's position as the sheriff would make some people doubt her qualifications, but she refused to let that stop her from helping Finn.

"Deputy Mercer has plenty of experience handling cases like this," she said, meeting Mr. Hutchinson's gaze. "I'm just here to assist him.

Besides, my sister, Sheriff Natalie Stone, wouldn't have put me in this position if she didn't trust me to uphold the law competently."

The moment the words left her lips, Sheila realized her mistake. A look of surprise crossed Mr. Hutchinson's face, his eyes glinting with newfound ammunition.

"Ah, so that's it—nepotism," he said. "What gives you the right to question my daughter?"

Before Sheila could respond, Officer Garner stepped forward, holding up a calming hand. "Come on, Roger," he said. "We're all here to find out what happened to Kristen and get justice for her, but we can't do that with you interrupting. The more you do that, the longer this process is going to take."

Roger snorted again and said nothing, watching to see what would happen next. Sheila hated the thought of conducting this interview under his disdainful gaze, but she had little choice.

She shifted her focus to Rita and Claire, trying to push away the lingering tension that Mr. Hutchinson's outburst had caused. She glanced at Finn, who gave a subtle nod, encouraging her to take the lead in questioning the girls. Surprised by his confidence in her, she felt both grateful and determined not to let him down.

"Can you please tell us, as simply as you can, what happened?" she asked the girls.

Rita remained quiet, her eyes downcast, but Claire stared straight into Sheila's eyes. "We were setting up for an event for our Psychology Club," she said. "We needed a box of masquerade masks for a game we were planning, but we couldn't find them, so I asked Rita to check the supply closet, just in case they were there."

As Claire recounted their story, Sheila observed the girls closely, noting Rita's fingers twisting nervously in her lap. She looked like she was reliving the memories in her mind, trapped there by the trauma of what she'd experienced.

Or is guilt part of it, too? Did she play some part in Lee's death?

"Rita went to check the supply closet, and when she came back, we noticed she'd tracked blood on the floor," Claire continued, sounding strangely matter-of-fact. "So, we followed the trail back to this dark hallway, and that's when we saw it—the blood dripping from a locker."

A shudder ran through Sheila as she pictured the horrific scene, imagining the fear and confusion the girls must have felt upon discovering Kristen's body. Despite her own discomfort, though, she knew she needed to keep probing to uncover any clues that might help solve the murder.

Sheila studied the faces of the two girls, trying to read their emotions as she asked her next question. "What did you do when you found the locker?"

Claire hesitated for a moment, her eyes glazing over as she relived the memory. "Rita opened it," she said finally, swallowing hard. "The body...it fell on her."

A chill ran down Sheila's spine at the image of Kristen's lifeless form collapsing onto the unsuspecting girl. She couldn't help but feel a pang of sympathy for Rita, who now seemed even more withdrawn and distraught than before.

"And what did you do next?" Sheila asked, hoping to keep the girls focused on recounting their experience.

"We ran and got help," Claire said. "That was all."

Not a word about moving the body. They must be lying, but why? What are they hiding?

"Rita," she began cautiously, "did you get blood on you when the body fell on you?"

Claire's eyes narrowed, and she spoke up again, seemingly intent on shielding her friend from further questioning. "Yes, she got blood on her. That's why we went to the restroom to clean up."

"And is that why you threw your sweatshirt into the trash?" Sheila asked, directing her question at Rita. Rita's eyes darted at hers in alarm, but the girl didn't answer.

"She wasn't trying to hide it, okay?" Claire said, sounding defensive. "She was just grossed out, wearing something with all that blood on it. I honestly didn't even remember that happened until you just mentioned it."

Sheila didn't buy this explanation for a second. Claire was hiding something—she could sense it in her bones.

"Did you go to the restroom before or after you told someone about the body?" Finn asked.

"Before," Claire replied, her voice tight.

Sheila studied Claire's face, noting the faint flush in her cheeks as she seemed to grow increasingly defensive. "Claire," she asked, trying to keep her voice steady and non-confrontational, "did you get near the body at all?"

"No," Claire answered quickly, a little too quickly for Sheila's liking.

"Would you mind showing me your hands, then?" Sheila asked.

"Absolutely not!" Roger interjected, his face turning red with anger. "Is she on trial now, or what? My daughter doesn't have to show anyone her hands!"

"Mr. Hutchinson, please," Officer Garner said. "Let them do their job."

Roger shook his head bitterly, but said nothing more.

Sheila met Claire's gaze again. "Claire, please show me your hands."

With a nervous glance at her father, Claire hesitated for a moment before finally holding out her hands for Sheila to see. They looked clean, not a trace of blood anywhere on them.

"There," Roger said triumphantly. "You believe her now?"

As Sheila scrutinized every inch of Claire's fingers, her gaze was drawn to the ring on the middle finger of Claire's right hand—a simple silver band adorned with a small blue stone that glinted under the fluorescent light.

"Could you remove your ring for me, please?" Sheila asked, her heart pounding in anticipation.

Claire's eyes widened, and she glanced down at the ring as if seeing it for the first time. She swallowed hard, then slowly slid it off her finger, revealing the piece of jewelry in its entirety.

Sheila took the ring from her, careful not to touch the inside of the band. As she turned it over in her hand, she noticed a faint reddish-brown stain on the inner surface. It was barely noticeable, but it was there.

Her palms suddenly felt clammy, and she had to force herself to maintain her composure as she handed the ring to Finn. She knew, without a doubt, that she was on the right track. The truth was within reach, and she was determined to uncover it.

Finn studied it in silence for a moment before nodding, his face giving away nothing.

"What?" Claire asked, as if unable to contain her curiosity any longer. "What's going on?"

Sheila held up the ring for Claire to see. "There's blood on the inside of this ring, Claire," she said, her voice steady despite the turmoil within her. "I know that you and Rita moved Kristen's body. What I want to understand is why."

Claire's eyes widened in denial, her lips parting as if to protest, but Rita interrupted, her voice barely more than a whisper. "We *did* move her." The relief in Rita's expression was palpable as she finally admitted the truth. "We thought maybe she was still alive. We wanted to get her to the hospital."

Sheila's gaze never left Claire's face, watching the nervous energy shift into something more vulnerable. She turned her attention back to Rita, noting the tremble in her hands.

"Why did you lie about it?" she asked.

Claire looked away, her lips pressed tightly together in an expression of stubborn defiance.

"We didn't want to get in trouble," Rita said. "As soon as we'd done it, we knew we should have just left her where she was. We...we panicked, you know?"

Sheila nodded, feeling a stirring of sympathy for what Rita had been through. "How long did it take to clean up after trying to move the body?" she asked.

"Maybe fifteen or twenty minutes," Rita replied, her eyes downcast.

Sheila's mind raced, piecing together the timeline. "That means you found Kristen at seven thirty, not seven forty-five as you originally claimed." She didn't know whether this difference would prove significant later on, but the more accurate a timetable they could get now, the better.

Rita nodded, tears glistening in her eyes. "We were scared. We didn't know what to do."

Claire shifted uncomfortably, biting her lip. Her expression of defiance was gone, replaced by something else—grief, maybe?

"I knew Kristen," she said softly. "We were on the volleyball team together."

Sheila felt a spark of understanding—as an athlete herself, she knew what it was like to form close bonds within a competitive environment. She leaned in, offering Claire a small nod. "I used to be a kickboxer," she said. "I know how intense those friendships can become."

Claire seemed to relax slightly, her shoulders easing from their tense hunch. She met Sheila's gaze and nodded. "Yeah, you get to know people pretty well when you're pushing yourselves to the limit together."

"Tell me more about your relationship with Kristen," Sheila said, sensing that Claire had more to share.

"Kristen was...she was amazing on the court," Claire began, her voice taking on a note of admiration. "She played like she had something to prove. And when we won, she made sure everyone knew we were the best."

"Sounds like she was quite the competitor," Sheila said, remembering her own drive to succeed in the sports world.

Claire nodded. "Coach Richards pushed all of us hard, but she saw something special in Kristen. I think that's why she was always getting on Kristen's case."

"Getting on her case?" Sheila asked, casting a troubled glance at Finn. "What do you mean?"

Claire shifted in her seat before continuing. "Well, Coach Richards could be pretty tough on all of us, but with Kristen...it was different. She would yell at her, sometimes even call her names. It was like she had it out for her."

Sheila's heart skipped a beat at the revelation. "Did Kristen ever talk to you about how she felt about Coach Richards?" she asked.

Claire hesitated, biting her lip. She glanced at Rita and then looked back at Sheila. "Not really, no. But I could tell it bothered her. Sometimes, after practice, she'd just sit there on the bench, staring at nothing. Like she was trying to figure out why Coach Richards was so hard on her."

"Did it ever escalate beyond words? Ever get physical?"

Claire hesitated. "This one time, Kristen talked back, told Coach Richards it was unfair how she was being treated. The two started arguing, and then Coach Richards shoved her. Kristen fell backward onto the court, and everyone just froze. It was like no one knew what to do."

Sheila's blood boiled at the thought of a coach physically harming a player. "Did anyone report it?" she asked.

Claire shook her head. "No. We all just kind of...pretended it didn't happen. Kristen didn't want to make a big deal out of it, so we respected that. I think she was embarrassed. Besides, it was just a shove—we all get a little out of hand sometimes, don't we?"

Sheila frowned, saying nothing. Was it possible there had been another incident between Kristen and Coach Richards, one that had gone much further than a shove?

One that had ended in blood?

CHAPTER FIVE

Sheila frowned as she knocked on the door to Coach Richards' office. She was still thinking of the conversation she'd had with Claire Hutchinson and Rita Cohen, and Claire's words about how hard Coach Richards had pushed Kristen Lee—even to the point of literally shoving her.

Was that simply fostering a competitive spirit in the players, or had there been genuine hostility involved? And what other lines might have been crossed when Claire wasn't around to see?

"Come in," a voice called, sounding a touch impatient. Sheila turned the doorknob and let herself in, with Finn close behind. The office was surprisingly neat, the walls lined with shelves filled with trophies and photographs of various volleyball teams. A large window allowed sunlight to filter in, illuminating the room and casting shadows on the hardwood floor. At the far end, behind a massive oak desk piled high with papers and sports-related paraphernalia, sat Coach Richards.

The stern-faced woman looked to be in her early fifties, with short-cropped, graying hair and a strong build that spoke of years spent coaching and playing sports herself. Her eyes bore into Sheila and Finn with an intensity that matched her reputation.

"Have a seat," Richards said, gesturing toward two chairs in front of her desk. Sheila couldn't help but feel like she was back in school herself, facing a headmistress for some minor infraction.

Sheila squared her shoulders, took a deep breath, and began. "Ms. Richards, my name is Sheila Stone, and this is Officer Finn Mercer. We're investigating the death of Kristen Lee."

The coach's eyes narrowed at the mention of Kristen's name, but she said nothing.

Sheila continued, "We'd like to ask you some questions about her, if that's all right."

"Fine," Richards replied curtly, her fingers drumming impatiently on the desk. "Fire away."

"What was your relationship to Kristen?" Sheila asked.

"My *relationship*?" Richards said, arching an eyebrow. "I was the coach and she was the player. Simple as that."

Sheila pursed her lips, composing herself. This was going to be more challenging than she'd thought.

"What kind of a player was she?" Sheila asked.

"Oh, she was an excellent volleyball player," Richards said, her voice softening ever so slightly. "She worked hard, never complained, and gave everything she had on the court." Her gaze shifted to the various team photos behind her, lingering on one where Kristen stood proudly among her teammates. "I'm very proud of my volleyball team, and it's devastating to lose a player like her."

Was the pain in the coach's eyes genuine, or just an act? Sheila couldn't tell, but either way, she sensed the woman was holding something back. She decided to probe a bit further.

"Did you notice any changes in Kristen's behavior recently?" she asked. "Anything that might have indicated she was going through a rough time?"

"Nothing out of the ordinary," Richards answered after a brief pause, her eyes flicking away from Sheila's probing stare. "Student-athletes like Kristen face a lot of pressure, but she seemed to handle it well."

In her mind, Sheila quickly reviewed Claire Hutchinson's words about Richards' tough attitude toward Kristen.

"Did you ever have any conflict with Kristen?" she asked.

"Of course," Richards said with a dismissive wave of her hand as she leaned back in her chair. "I push all my athletes hard because I believe in their potential, and sometimes that leads to...friction. Kristen was no exception."

"So you weren't particularly hard on Kristen?"

"Kristen had an immense talent," Coach Richards replied, her eyes narrowing slightly. "I saw great potential in her, and I wanted her to reach it. Sometimes, people learn best when they're doubted rather than praised. It forces them to dig deep and prove themselves."

Sheila took in the tense lines around the coach's eyes and the way her fingers drummed on the desk. She remembered her own experiences as a Division One athlete, feeling the pressure from coaches who seemed to expect perfection. Her next question felt risky, but she had to ask.

"Coach, we heard about an incident where you supposedly shoved Kristen during practice. Is that true?"

The color drained from Richards' face, and she shot up from her chair, her hands gripping the edge of her desk. "That's preposterous! I would never lay a hand on one of my players. Who told you such a thing?"

"I'm not at liberty to share that," Sheila replied, her heart racing at the sudden change in the coach's demeanor.

"Well, rumors are dangerous," Richards hissed, leaning forward. "They can ruin lives and reputations. So don't go spreading lies about me or my players."

Sheila held the coach's gaze, not backing down. Still, she knew there was no point in pushing this line of questioning any further. The coach's defensiveness spoke volumes, but without concrete evidence, it was best to tread lightly.

"Of course," she said, her voice steady and calm. "We're just trying to put the pieces together and find out what happened to Kristen."

"Then I suggest you focus on facts," Richards snapped, sinking back into her chair, her face a mask of anger.

Taking a deep breath to regain her composure, Sheila glanced at Finn, who had been quiet throughout the exchange. He cleared his throat and spoke up.

"Coach Richards, did you notice any changes in Kristen's behavior lately? Was she acting differently or struggling with anything in particular?"

The coach seemed to consider the question carefully before answering. "Well, I can't say for sure, but I knew she was dealing with some personal issues. She didn't share any details with me, though."

Sheila's brow furrowed as she noted the evasive answer. She wondered if Richards was hiding something or simply respecting Kristen's privacy.

"Did anyone have a reason to hurt Kristen?" Sheila asked, her eyes locked onto Richards', trying to gauge her reaction.

For just a moment, the coach hesitated, her gaze flickering away from Sheila's. Then, she straightened her back and met Sheila's eyes once more. "No," she said firmly. "I can't think of anyone who would want to hurt her."

Sheila felt a twinge of suspicion, but without any proof, there was no point in confronting Richards about her possible lies. Instead, she nodded, letting the matter rest for now. Her instincts told her that there was more to this story, and she was determined to find out what it was.

"Is that all?" Richards asked. "I really am very busy, and most of these questions would be better directed to Kristen's friends and family."

Sheila nodded, sensing they had learned all they would from the coach—for now, at least. "Of course," she said, forcing a polite smile. "Thank you for your time. Let us know if you think of anything else."

"I'll do that," Richards said. "And in return, all I ask is that you don't go around repeating things that aren't true. There's no telling how much harm it can do."

"We understand," Finn said. "Thank you again for your time."

Sheila and Finn stepped out into the hallway, the sound of their footsteps sharp against the linoleum floor. The fluorescent lights cast a cold glow over them as they walked away from Coach Richards' office.

"Something's not right," Sheila said quietly, her brow furrowed in thought. "She's lying."

Finn glanced at her, his eyes narrowing. "Why would she lie?"

"Maybe she's covering for someone." Sheila's mind raced, recalling her own experiences in sports. "Coaches sometimes cover for star athletes, especially when it comes to issues that could hurt the team."

"You think Coach Richards is actually protecting Kristen?"

"I don't know, but it's a possibility. Kristen Lee is the victim here, there's no doubt about that...but maybe it didn't start that way. Maybe someone was settling a score."

CHAPTER SIX

The harsh fluorescent lights above cast a somber glow on the gathered crowd of students, their wide eyes and downturned mouths reflecting shock and grief. Reagan stood among them, taking in the crime scene at Coldwater Community College with a detached interest that belied a racing heart.

Pathetic, Reagan thought. *Don't they all know what kind of person she was?*

"Such a tragedy," whispered a girl beside Reagan, dabbing at her tear-streaked cheeks with a crumpled tissue. "Kristen Lee...she was so talented."

The name hung heavy in the air, a weighty reminder of the basketball player whose life had been snuffed out so suddenly. Her body had been discovered in her locker earlier that day, a gruesome sight that had sent ripples of horror throughout the campus. The students huddled together, seeking solace in shared pain and whispered condolences.

Reagan, however, wasn't seeking solace. Reagan was here for the same reason one visits a foreign country: to try to imagine what it would be like to be somebody else.

That, and to enjoy the knowledge that justice had been served.

"Excuse me," a gruff voice interrupted Reagan's observations. A police officer approached, his uniform crisp and authoritative. His gaze was firm, unrelenting.

"I'm Officer Daniels," he said. "We're questioning anyone who might have any information about Kristen Lee. Did you know her?"

Reagan felt a chill, like icy fingers tracing a path along the vertebrae. "No, I didn't know her. We never crossed paths."

"Really?" Officer Daniels frowned, his brow furrowing as he studied Reagan's face. "What's your name?"

"Reagan. It's my middle name." Reagan expected the officer to ask for a full name, something Reagan was reluctant to give, but surprisingly the officer didn't ask for more.

"Well, Reagan," he said, "you seem awfully interested in what's going on here."

"Can you blame me?" Reagan replied, forcing a weak smile. "This is terrifying. I guess I'm just trying to understand how something like this could happen."

Why is he staring at me like that? Reagan thought. *Does he know who I am?* Reagan had to resist the urge to look down, afraid there might be a telltale drop of blood – on a sneaker, or perhaps staining the front of the jeans – to betray the truth of what had really happened.

The chilly air around the crime scene seemed to grow colder, making Reagan shiver involuntarily.

"Are you a student here at Coldwater?" Officer Daniels asked, his tone professional but tinged with just the slightest hint of suspicion.

"Uh, yes," Reagan stammered, palms growing sweaty. "I am."

"Which program are you enrolled in?" the officer pressed, narrowing his eyes as if expecting Reagan to falter.

"Graphic design," Reagan said. Reagan had always been good at improvisation, but still, the pressure of the moment was intense.

What if he realizes the truth? He can't prove anything, but if they turn the spotlight of the investigation on me...

"Really? That's interesting," Officer Daniels said, trying to sound conversational but unable to hide that note of skepticism. "How long have you been studying it for?"

"Two years," Reagan said, feigning confidence. Inside, however, Reagan's mind was screaming at her. *What the hell do you know about graphic design? What are you thinking?*

"Tell me," Officer Daniels went on, leaning in closer, his breath warm and sour against Reagan's face, "have you noticed anything unusual lately? Strange people hanging around, or maybe someone acting out of character?"

Reagan hesitated, weighing the options. It was tempting to fabricate a story, to divert attention toward someone else. But something told Reagan that Officer Daniels would see through such deception. Better to go with honesty, albeit a selective version of it.

"Nothing really stands out, no," Reagan admitted, shrugging nonchalantly. "It's just...I never thought something like this could happen here, you know? Everyone's so shaken up."

"Indeed," Officer Daniels said, stepping back as he surveyed the somber faces of the other students. "We'll find whoever did this, though. I promise you that." He gave Reagan a long stare as he said this.

The pulse in Reagan's ears was loud, crowding out all thoughts. *Come on, already. Don't you have better things to do?*

Just then a voice called out, shattering the tenuous silence. "Officer Daniels!"

Officer Daniels' head snapped up, his attention momentarily diverted by a distressed college staff member gesturing frantically toward an angry-looking man fighting his way through the students—the victim's father, presumably.

Seizing the opportunity, Reagan slipped away from the officer's penetrating gaze, disappearing into the shadows of a quiet hallway.

The fluorescent lights above flickered, casting an eerie glow on the linoleum floors as Reagan's footsteps echoed softly. Each step was filled with a mix of terror and exhilaration. This was a dangerous game, a dance on the knife's edge between freedom and capture.

And Reagan was loving every moment of it.

"Can you believe what happened?" a hushed voice whispered, the voice slipping out through a cracked door and momentarily distracting Reagan.

Reagan paused, curiosity piqued, and pressed against the cool wall, straining to catch every word of the conversation unfolding behind the closed door.

"Kristen didn't deserve this. She was so nice to everyone," the first voice continued, choking back a sob.

"Who could have done such a thing?" the second voice asked, her tone laced with disbelief and horror.

Reagan's lips curled into a small, satisfied smile. Fear was spreading like wildfire, just as Reagan had hoped, and the world would soon understand the consequences of Kristen Lee's actions. It was only a matter of time before someone made the connection.

And if they didn't—well, then Reagan would just have to make the connection for them. In the depths of Reagan's soul, a dark, insidious desire burned—the desire to be caught, to make the world understand the reasons that had led to such desperate measures. But for now, Reagan would remain a shadow, unseen and unheard, weaving an intricate web of fear and suspense.

And Kristen Lee and Jane Johnson would not be the only people caught in that web.

Continuing down the hallway, Reagan headed toward an exit and stepped out into the cool morning. The air was redolent with the scent of damp leaves and freshly cut grass. Police officers milled about, their movements slow and methodical, but Reagan could sense the lack of progress in the investigation. Reagan felt a pang of surprise, followed by a surge of confidence.

A hushed voice caught Reagan's attention. "It just doesn't make any sense."

A group of female students stood nearby, their faces pale and somber, engaged in a whispered conversation. Reagan edged closer, straining to hear their words while maintaining a casual demeanor.

"Who do you think is next?" another asked, her eyes darting nervously around the group.

Reagan's heart raced at the realization that this plan was working better than anticipated. Fear had taken root, and the seeds of anxiety were sprouting like weeds. Reagan couldn't help but feel a grim satisfaction at the thought.

"Should we talk to the police?" asked a tall girl with dark hair, her brow furrowed in concern.

"About what?" a blonde retorted, her arms crossed defensively over her chest. "We don't know anything, so what would be the point?"

"But we knew Kristen," the tall girl replied, her tone uncertain. "Maybe we know something important without knowing what it is."

Reagan listened to the exchange, drawn by the tall girl's sense of duty. *Why not toy with them? Maybe feed them a little misinformation? It would be so satisfying, seeing their fear up close.*

In the end, however, caution prevailed over temptation. Reagan knew that getting too involved would only increase the chances of being caught.

Then, as the group of female students started moving together, Reagan's eyes locked onto one girl in particular. She was petite with auburn hair and a confident stride that screamed arrogance. Reagan's heart clenched with bitterness.

Time to face the music, Reagan thought, pushing off from the wall and following the group. Reagan trailed like a shadow, maintaining enough distance to avoid arousing suspicion but sticking close enough that there was no fear of losing them.

"Hey, Sophie!" a voice called out, causing Reagan to tense momentarily. A lanky guy with glasses approached the auburn-haired girl, offering her a timid smile. "Ready for that study session we talked about?"

"Sure, Todd," she replied, returning the smile with a hint of...what...seduction? As they walked away together, Reagan couldn't help but notice the way Sophie's hand lingered on Todd's arm just a moment too long, a calculated gesture designed to manipulate the unsuspecting boy.

Playing with people's emotions like they're toys, Reagan thought angrily. *You won't get away with it for long.*

The pair entered a building, and Reagan followed suit, taking care to blend in with the throngs of students traversing the halls.

"Let's head to the library," Sophie suggested as she guided Todd down a corridor. "That's where you're supposed to 'study,' right?" Her eyes twinkled.

Todd nodded, casting an adoring glance in her direction. "Oh, yes," he answered playfully. "I've done plenty of 'studying' in the library."

Pathetic, Reagan thought with disdain, watching the interaction without staring directly at them. *A girl's just been murdered, and all these two can think about is fooling around. Sophie's even worse than I thought.*

The scent of old books and fresh ink wafted through the air, mingling with the murmurs of students exchanging idle gossip. The library loomed just ahead, an imposing structure that seemed to watch them with an air of silent judgment.

"Todd, I'm serious," Sophie was saying, playfully nudging her companion. "You should try out for the drama club. You'd be amazing!"

"Really?" Todd asked skeptically, his eyes lighting up with a mixture of hope and disbelief. "You think so?"

"Absolutely," she said, a wicked smile spreading across her face like a spider weaving its web.

Reagan couldn't believe how easily Sophie manipulated those around her. It sickened Reagan. Soon enough, however, Sophie would pay.

Today, if Reagan could find a way to isolate the girl.

"Here we are," Sophie announced, pushing open the heavy wooden doors of the library. The hushed atmosphere inside enveloped them like a blanket, muffling the sounds of the outside world.

"It's like a graveyard in here," Todd said.

"Shh," Sophie scolded teasingly, placing a slender finger against her lips. "We don't want to disturb anyone. We have so much work to do."

The two giggled. As they made their way further into the library, Reagan kept close watch on them, expertly navigating the maze of towering bookshelves and blending seamlessly into the shadows.

"Over here, Todd," Sophie said, leading him toward a secluded corner nestled between two rows of ancient tomes. "This looks like a pretty good place, don't you think?"

"Oh, yes," Todd said. "Perfect." With that, he slipped his arms around Sophie and pressed his lips hungrily against hers.

Reagan watched with disgust as the two lost themselves in each other. For a moment, Reagan considered taking both of them—it would be fitting, wouldn't it, catching them at their most vulnerable? But no, Todd hadn't done anything wrong, other than being a selfish, immature idiot.

Sophie was the real prize.

But how was Reagan supposed to get to her if Todd wouldn't leave her alone?

The kissing intensified, and Sophie stole a look around to make sure they were alone. Reagan darted out of view, hiding behind a bookshelf. *Did she see me? And if she did, would she have any idea why I'm here?*

Suddenly this whole plan seemed far too risky, far too dangerous. Reagan was playing with fire, risking getting caught, and there was too much to do before that happened, if it happened at all.

Besides, even if she got past Todd, how would Reagan deal with all the police patrolling the campus? Maybe it would be better to go somewhere else.

Then Reagan had an idea.

I'll just have to leave for a while, come back for Sophie later when things have calmed down. In the meantime...

In the meantime, there were other campuses, other students.

Stealing one last glimpse at the kissing couple, Reagan stole away, hurrying between the bookshelves and heading toward the door.

So much to do, Reagan thought, *and so little time.*

CHAPTER SEVEN

"I thought we'd be able to search for these electronically," Sheila said, trying not to grow frustrated by the tedious task before them. She pulled out yet another out-of-place folder and set it aside. "Whoever 'organized' these files should go to jail."

The morning sun cast a soft glow through the blinds of the principal's office at Coldwater Community College. Sheila Stone stood with Finn Mercer, surrounded by towering metal cabinets filled to the brim with disciplinary records. She frowned, running her fingers along dusty files as she tried to locate anything related to Kristen Lee, whose lifeless body had been found in her locker just hours earlier that morning.

"Welcome to the thrilling world of police work," Finn said, his lips curving into a wry smile. "It's not always car chases and shootouts."

"Is that supposed to make me feel better?" Sheila asked, shooting him a playful glare. She returned her focus to the pile in front of her, carefully scanning the labels on each file before setting them aside with increasing impatience.

The principal's office was spacious, yet cluttered. A large wooden desk dominated one corner, stacks of papers covering its polished surface. Various awards and certificates lined the walls, while diplomas hung proudly above the desk. The scent of stale coffee lingered in the air, mingling with the musty odor of well-worn leather from the chairs scattered around the room.

With the principal out addressing the worried students, Sheila and Finn were making use of the rare opportunity to sift through the confidential files. The principal had given them permission to do this (sneaking in here on their own would have been a significant breach of confidentiality, not to mention the fact that anything they found would not have been usable in a court of law), but he had insisted he could not join them, citing the need to "tend to" his students, a turn of phrase that, in Sheila's mind, made him sound like a shepherd looking after a flock of wandering sheep.

which might, she supposed, not be too far from the mark.

As Sheila pulled open one of the creaky drawers, a wave of nostalgia washed over her. It reminded her of when she used to sneak into her coach's office back in high school, searching for any hints about the upcoming kickboxing competitions. She had been something of a trouble-maker that way. Perhaps it had been her way of rebelling, since she never felt she could live up to the standard set by her sister.

"Any luck?" Finn asked, breaking her reverie.

"Nothing yet," she admitted, suppressing a sigh.

Her fingers traced the edges of the disorganized files, her brows furrowing in frustration. The principal's office was a mixture of old-school charm and modern touches, but it seemed that the filing system had been left in the past. How anyone was supposed to find what they were looking for in that sea of papers was beyond her.

"So," Finn said casually, "how are you liking police work?"

Sheila paused, considering his question. Her kickboxing career was probably over, since no trainer would want to risk her dying in the ring due to the brain injury she'd sustained in her last match, and she couldn't deny that the adrenaline rush from being involved in a real-life murder investigation had reignited a spark in her.

"I'm enjoying it," she said, her eyes flicking up to meet Finn's gaze. "But I'm keeping my options open. Why do you think I have what it takes to be a good police officer?" She said it playfully, as if it were a joke, but Finn seemed to take it seriously.

He studied her for a moment, his blue eyes thoughtful. "If you're anything like your sister, then definitely. She's one of the best cops I know. And you, Sheila, have the makings of an excellent police officer."

Sheila felt a warmth spread through her chest at his words. Did he really believe that, or was he just trying to encourage her? And would anyone ever praise her for her own merits, without in some way comparing her to Natlaie?

Her fingers grazed over the worn edges of the files, her thoughts drifting to her sister. She hesitated for a moment, then glanced at Finn. "Speaking of Natalie, has she talked to you about what happened?"

Finn looked up from a file in his hands, confusion furrowing his brow. "What do you mean?"

"About the shooting," Sheila said, feeling a knot tighten in her stomach. "Sometimes I feel like she blames me for it."

Finn was quiet for a few moments, the rustling of papers the only sound in the room. Eventually, he sighed. "I don't think Natalie knows what to make of what happened," he said. "She's a strong person, and she's used to being able to rely on herself. Having to rely on others is very difficult for her."

Sheila noticed that Finn hadn't exactly answered her question. Before she could ask a follow-up question, however, her gaze fell on a file with Kristen Lee's name scrawled across the tab. "Hey, look at this," she said, pulling it out and waving it at Finn.

Finn moved closer, and together they opened the file. Inside were several complaints lodged against Lee for bullying. One girl claimed Lee had spread nasty rumors about her after a failed attempt to join the volleyball team; another described how Lee had stolen her clothes from the locker room, forcing her to walk home in just her gym uniform.

"Seems like Kristen had a habit of picking on other girls, especially non-athletes," Finn said, his brow creasing as he read over the pages.

Sheila nodded, feeling a chill run down her spine. Having been a scrawny little girl when she first started kickboxing, she knew firsthand how difficult it could be to stand up against someone stronger or more skilled—especially when they abused their power. The thought of anyone suffering at the hands of a bully made her blood boil.

As she scanned the document, one particular complaint caught her eye. The words 'hazing incident' jumped from the page, and she felt a knot in her stomach. "Finn, look at this," she said, pointing to the paragraph.

"What does it say?" Finn asked, his eyes narrowing as he leaned in to read alongside her.

"Kristen Lee was involved in a hazing incident a few months ago," Sheila said. "She was one of the ringleaders in a group of volleyball players who took things too far with a freshman named Lila Hartlett. They forced her to run through an obstacle course they'd set up in the gym, but with a twist—they'd covered the floor with slippery oil."

"Doesn't sound so terrible," Finn said.

"Wait till you hear the rest. Apparently, Lila fell hard and broke her leg in three places. Kristen and the others were suspended for a week, but that's all the punishment they seemed to have received."

"Could Lila have wanted revenge on Kristen?" Finn asked. "The incident was several months ago, so maybe she's recovered from the injury by now."

Sheila chewed her lip thoughtfully, considering Finn's words. If Lila truly held resentment toward Kristen, she might not have been happy with the slap on the wrist Kristen had received.

She might have even decided to take matters into her own hands.

CHAPTER EIGHT

Sheila said nothing as she walked alongside Finn Mercer down the hallway, heading toward the dorm hall where Lila Hartlett had recently come to live again after convalescing at home for several months. She was thinking about the nature of justice and how Lila must have felt knowing that Kristen Lee had essentially gotten a slap on the wrist for a hazing that had resulted in a broken leg for Lila.

I'd be angry, too, Sheila thought. *It doesn't mean I'd stab Kristen to death and stuff her in her locker...but I'd want her to pay* somehow.

The faint scent of disinfectant and stale pizza lingered in the air as they passed rows of closed doors, each one adorned with a whiteboard scribbled with messages and doodles. The flickering fluorescent lights above cast eerie shadows on the beige linoleum floor below their feet.

As they reached their destination, Sheila couldn't help but feel a pang of nostalgia for her own college days, which now seemed a lifetime away. The door they stopped at was covered in various slogans and pictures—"Save the Earth" written in bold, colorful letters; a peace sign drawn with meticulous detail; and a quote from some obscure poet she couldn't quite place.

The muffled sound of soft voices seeped through the thin door, drawing Sheila's attention back to the present moment. She raised her hand and gave a firm knock, causing the whispers to abruptly cease. After a brief silence, the door creaked open, revealing a young woman who appeared both troubled and surprised by their presence.

"Can I help you?" she asked cautiously, her wide eyes darting between Sheila and Finn.

"Hi," Sheila said, offering a warm smile that didn't quite reach her eyes. "I'm Sheila Stone, and this is Officer Finn Mercer. We're looking for Lila Hartlett."

The young woman hesitated, biting her lower lip nervously. Her unkempt hair hung in loose waves around her face, framing high cheekbones and a scattering of freckles across her nose. Her eyes, an unusual shade of gray, held a mixture of vulnerability and defiance that intrigued Sheila.

"That's me," she finally said. "Is this about the murder?"

"Let's talk inside if that's okay with you," Finn said.

"Sure," Lila agreed, stepping back and allowing them to enter the dorm hall.

They stepped into a spacious common area, where a few other girls were milling about, their curious gazes fixated on Sheila and Finn. As if sensing they might be questioned next if they stuck around, they quickly dispersed, leaving the trio alone in the room.

The dorm hall was furnished with mismatched sofas and chairs, arranged haphazardly around a low wooden table covered in textbooks and empty snack wrappers. The space had a lived-in quality that reminded Sheila of the countless hours she'd spent studying and socializing in her own college dormitory. A row of doors lined one wall, each bearing a nameplate and a collection of hastily scribbled notes. One door, in particular, caught Sheila's eye—the one with "Lila" scrawled across it in bold, looping letters.

"Please, have a seat," Lila said, gesturing toward the worn sofas. Her eyes darted nervously around the room, betraying her unease. Sheila couldn't help but feel a pang of sympathy for the girl—she was clearly uncomfortable with law enforcement barging into her safe space.

As they settled onto the couches, Sheila noted the small kitchenette tucked away in one corner of the room. It was cluttered with dishes and half-empty food containers, evidence of endless late-night study sessions and hurried meals on the go. The sight made her stomach churn with nostalgia.

"There's water heating up, if you want some tea in a few minutes," Lila said, clearly trying to be a good hostess despite the circumstances.

Sheila watched Lila's unsteady gait as she limped toward a nearby chair. "How's your leg?" she asked.

Lila winced, her fingers subconsciously skimming the edge of her jeans where the injury lay hidden. "It still hurts, but it's getting better. I'm hopeful for a full recovery." She gave Sheila a tight-lipped smile. "It was just an accident."

Sheila studied Lila's face, searching for any telltale signs of deceit. The girl's eyes darted away, a flicker of something unreadable passing across her expression. In a soft, empathetic tone, Sheila pressed on. "Was it really an accident, Lila?"

A tense silence filled the room, Finn shifting in his seat while Lila's knuckles turned white from gripping the chair. Finally, she exhaled shakily and admitted, "No. It wasn't an accident. I...I was involved in a dangerous hazing ritual last year, and that's how I got hurt. This stupid obstacle course they made me run." Her voice trembled with emotion, bitterness seeping into each word. "I had to take months off from school just to recover."

Sheila could hear the resentment, the pain, in Lila's confession. As an athlete, she understood all too well the frustration of being sidelined by an injury, especially one that wasn't your fault. She empathized with the young woman before her, but she couldn't let her feelings cloud her judgment. There was still a murder to solve.

"That must've been difficult," Sheila said. "Just when you're starting to get settled in. You're a freshman, is that right?"

Lila nodded. Then, her eyes seemed to drift back to a time long past, and her voice softened as she began to speak. "I grew up in a small town, so isolated that we didn't even have a single traffic light. Everyone knew everyone else's business, and there was no room for personal growth or being different."

She stared out the window at the bustling college campus, as if seeing her past life play out before her eyes. "Coming here to Coldwater Community College was my chance to break free, make friends, and finally experience life beyond the confines of my hometown. That's why I figured the hazing would be harmless—just a silly rite of passage. I never thought it could end like this." She looked down at her injured leg as if it were a tangible reminder of her shattered dreams.

Sheila, sensing the depth of Lila's pain, pressed on with her questions. "What role did Kristen Lee play in all of this?"

The bitterness in Lila's expression intensified, and her words came out sharp and biting. "Kristen was the ringleader. She orchestrated the whole thing, made sure I couldn't back out. It was like a sick game to her, and I was just her pawn." Her hands clenched into fists, and Sheila could see her knuckles turning white. "Now that she's dead, I know I'm supposed to feel grief or sadness, but honestly? All I feel is relief. At least now, she can't hurt anyone else."

The intensity of Lila's emotions made it clear that Kristen's death had brought some sort of closure for her. But did that mean she'd played a part in it?

Finn, watching Lila's face closely, ventured a question. "Did you ever confront Kristen about the hazing?"

Lila shook her head, her lips pressed into a thin line. "No. There would've been no point. Kristen would never have taken responsibility for her actions. She thrived on power and control." Her eyes darkened with frustration. "I tried to get the school involved, but the principal dismissed it as 'hearsay.' Said there was no proof of what happened." She snorted. "It's amazing—there are so many cameras on this campus, yet somehow they all missed what happened to me."

Sheila studied Lila's face, searching for any hint of deception or hidden intent. It seemed plausible that someone like Lila, strong-willed and determined, might have decided to take matters into her own hands. But would she be capable of killing Kristen? Sheila recalled Lila's earlier limp and wondered if she was strong enough to lift Kristen's body into the locker.

One way or another, she knew she had to probe deeper. "So," she said, "after the hazing incident, did you keep your distance from Kristen and her friends?"

"Of course," Lila said, crossing her arms defensively. "I didn't want anything to do with them anymore. I focused on my recovery and my studies. That was all I could do."

"Did you ever fantasize about getting back at Kristen for what she did to you?" Sheila asked, looking straight into Lila's eyes.

For a moment, Lila hesitated, then let out a resigned sigh. "I'd be lying if I said I didn't. But it was just that—a fantasy. I never acted on it." She met Sheila's gaze, her eyes pleading for understanding. "You have to believe me. I wouldn't have gone that far."

Sheila considered Lila's words carefully, weighing them against her instincts and the cold, hard facts of the case. She couldn't shake the feeling that Lila might still be hiding something—but for now, there was nothing more to be gained from pushing further.

The shrill sound of the tea kettle pierced the tense atmosphere, and Lila made a move to stand up. Sheila held up her hand to stop her. "I'll take care of it," she said with a small smile.

As Sheila headed to the kitchen, she looked over Lila's shoulder and caught Finn's eye. She tapped her thumb against her four fingers, pantomiming speech. *Keep her talking,* she mouthed. Finn nodded.

"You must have been devastated, getting injured like that," he said to Lila.

She nodded. "I couldn't believe it. My feet just slipped out from under me, and then there was that crack..."

The conversation faded into the background of Sheila's thoughts as she focused on pouring tea into the mug sitting on the counter, a bag with some kind of herbal blend inside already waiting to be steeped.

Her mind raced as she considered the possibility that Lila might be involved in Kristen's murder. She needed more information, something solid that could either confirm or dispel her suspicions.

Her gaze lingered on the slightly ajar door to Lila's bedroom, and an idea formed. With a quick glance back at Finn and Lila, she silently made her way into the room.

The interior of Lila's bedroom was neat and organized, giving off a sense of discipline that seemed to mirror its occupant. The walls were adorned with motivational posters and a few personal touches—a framed photo of Lila with her parents, a sketch of what appeared to be a childhood home. A row of textbooks lined the desk, each meticulously labeled with color-coded sticky notes.

Sheila's eyes scanned the room, searching for any indication of Lila's involvement in the murder. She knew she didn't have much time, so she focused on the most likely places for evidence: desk drawers, a small wastebasket, and finally, Lila's phone, which lay charging on the nightstand.

To her surprise, the phone was unlocked, the screen displaying a chain of text messages from around seven that morning. As Sheila skimmed through the conversation, her heart rate slowed, and her shoulders relaxed. The texts revealed a light-hearted exchange between Lila and her boyfriend, full of flirtatious banter and talk of weekend plans. The conversation had gone back and forth every minute or two for most of an hour, and it seemed highly unlikely that Lila could have been involved in Kristen's murder while carrying on this conversation.

Sheila let out a quiet breath she hadn't realized she'd been holding and slipped back out of the room, the phone left exactly as she had found it.

She picked Lila's mug and carried it to the other room. The steam swirled above the mug like a miniature tornado, and the scent of chamomile filled her nostrils. She handed the mug to Lila, who eyed her with an inquisitive expression.

"What took you so long?" she asked, arching an eyebrow.

"Couldn't find the honey," Sheila said, hiding her true intentions behind a casual smile. "Thought you might want some."

"It's in the cabinet above the sink." Lila was frowning at her, as if sensing she was missing something.

Finn sighed and rose. "Well, we won't take up any more of your time, Miss Hartlett. Thank you for talking with us."

"Of course," Lila said, setting her tea down on a nearby table. "If there's anything else I can do to help, just let me know."

Sheila and Finn exchanged glances before nodding their thanks once more and heading out of the dorm room. As soon as the door closed behind them, Finn turned to Sheila, curiosity burning in his eyes.

"Did you find anything in her room?" he said

"Nothing that points to her being involved in Kristen's murder," Sheila said, her gaze lingering on the closed door. "But something's been bothering me since we spoke to her."

"Which is?"

"Remember how Lila mentioned the security cameras on campus? I think we should look into getting footage from early this morning—maybe last night, too."

"You don't think the killer would have been careful to avoid cameras?"

"I think this was largely a crime of passion—you don't stab someone that many times unless you're really worked up about something. And when you're that emotional..." She clenched her jaw, hoping she was on to something. "The last thing you're thinking about is covering your tracks."

CHAPTER NINE

Sheila sat hunched over the computer screen, her eyes scanning the security footage from Coldwater Community College. Beside her, Deputy Finn Mercer leaned in, his brow furrowed in concentration.

"There's got to be something here," Sheila muttered. "If only we knew what we were looking for."

The sheriff's department buzzed with activity around them. The sound of ringing phones, the distant hum of a copier machine, and the muted conversations of other officers made it hard to concentrate. Sheila could smell the lingering aroma of burnt coffee mingling with the unmistakable scent of disinfectant. It took her back to the first time she'd set foot in this place, when everything had seemed so foreign and intimidating. Now, these sights, sounds, and smells were becoming familiar, almost comforting.

"Look at this," she said, pointing at the screen. "Around seven-thirty this morning, right after Rita and Claire found Kristen's body. In the background, you can just barely see the girls walking by—on their way to the restroom to clean up, by the look of it. Doesn't tell us anything new, but it does confirm their story."

"Good catch," Finn said. As he leaned closer, a small compass, attached to a paracord looped around his neck, dangled in front of him. The compass looked old and beat-up, as if it had traveled the world and seen its share of adventures.

Finn caught Sheila looking at the compass, and he hurriedly straightened, scooping the compass up and slipping it back into his shirt. He cleared his throat.

"You know," he said suddenly, "you're getting pretty good at this detective stuff, Sheila."

Ordinarily, such praise would have meant a great deal to Sheila. Just now, however, it seemed clear to her that Finn was simply trying to deflect from something else. But what? Was there something about the compass he didn't want her to know? Was it too personal to him to talk about?

"Thanks," she said, smiling but feeling utterly fake.

Should I just ask him about it? she wondered. *No, he clearly doesn't want to talk about it. If I push him, he'll just change the subject—and perhaps be even more resistant from talking about it in the future. Better to let him tell me in his own time.*

She didn't know whether that time would ever come, but if she became a full-time police officer, and if she and Finn ended up working together, she hoped that he would eventually learn to trust her.

Even with his secrets.

Her eyes narrowed as she scanned the video feed, her fingers tapping a rhythm against the keyboard. The thumb drive contained the last forty-eight hours of footage, and considering the fact that there were more than thirty cameras sprinkled across Coldwater Community College's campus, wading through the sea of information was a daunting task.

"So how does this compare to your kickboxing days?" Finn asked, breaking the silence between them. "Your sister never talked much about the ring."

Sheila paused the video and looked over at Finn, considering his question. She tried to take her mind off the necklace, focusing instead on his question. "They're different, but there are similarities, too," she said. "Both require determination, focus, and adaptability. With kickboxing, you need to read your opponent's movements and find their weaknesses. In a way, that's what we're doing now—analyzing the footage to find any cracks in the case."

Finn leaned back in his chair, an intrigued expression crossing his face. "That's an interesting way to look at it. So, do you miss competing?"

"Sometimes," she said. "But solving cases like this one gives me a different kind of fulfillment. It's not just about winning; it's about bringing justice and closure to people who need it most."

Finn nodded thoughtfully, and Sheila found herself wanting to know more about him in return. "So, how long have you been a deputy?" she asked.

"Eight years," he said, his gaze fixed on the screen. "Feels like a lifetime, sometimes."

"Do you like it? Your job, I mean."

He shrugged. "It pays the bills. But more importantly, it's a chance to make a difference, you know? Help people when they need it most."

Sheila couldn't help but be impressed by his dedication. "But why haven't you tried to climb the ranks? With your experience, I'd think you would've advanced by now."

"Never cared for the politics," Finn admitted with a wry smile. "I just want to do my job and go home at the end of the day, knowing I helped serve the cause of justice. Climbing the ladder often means playing games I have no interest in."

Despite Finn's smile, Sheila sensed there was more to this than he was saying. She found herself curious to know what he was hiding, and she sensed he was a man who had grown accustomed to his own secrets, comfortable keeping counsel with himself. She admired that independence, and she found herself trying to come up with a tactful way to ask if there was more he wasn't saying.

"Besides," he continued before she could think of what to say, "I get a gun and a badge. Tough to complain about that."

Sheila snorted. "Meanwhile, I don't even have a pair of handcuffs. What happens if I'm alone with a suspect and need to detain them?"

Finn raised an eyebrow at her. "Isn't that what an arm lock is for?"

"Yeah, so I can get sued for dislocating someone's shoulder? No thanks."

Finn chuckled and pulled a pair of handcuffs from his belt. "You want them so bad? Here you go. I'll pick up another pair for myself later."

Sheila held the handcuffs in the air for a moment, thinking how surreal the moment felt. It was one thing to work with the police, study crime scenes, and interview witnesses and suspects. It was something else entirely to carry around a symbol of authority like a pair of handcuffs.

"You'll get used to them," Finn said, as if reading her mind. "Just another accessory to carry around."

As Sheila was pondering Finn's words, wondering if she would indeed one day become as familiar with the tools of the police officer's trade as he was, something from the footage caught her eye. She paused the video and rewound it slightly.

"Look at this," she said, pointing to a female student lingering near the lockers where Kristen Lee's body had been found. The girl seemed nervous, glancing around furtively as if expecting someone to catch her in the act.

"And who might you be, miss?" Finn murmured, leaning closer to the screen.

Sheila let the video play, and the nervous student walked off. quickly disappearing from view. She tried to find the girl on another camera but was unable to do so.

"I wonder where she went," she murmured.

"Maybe we're doing it backwards," Finn said. "Maybe instead of looking for her, we should look for Kristen Lee. If this girl killed her, I have a feeling we might see her around Kristen, maybe lurking in the background or watching from a distance."

Sheila nodded, liking the plan. She quickly scanned through the footage, rewinding and fast-forwarding until she found a clip of Kristen Lee from the previous evening. She watched as Kristen walked down the hallway, her backpack slung over one shoulder and her headphones in her ears, completely unaware of the fate she would soon face.

Kristen soon reached her dorm hall and slipped inside. Sheila was about to switch feeds. Then, on instinct, she decided to stay where she was and accelerate the playback speed. About fifteen minutes after Kristen had gone into her room, the nervous-looking girl they'd seen earlier showed up, pacing in front of the door, her fists clenching and unclenching in an unmistakable display of anger.

"Sure looks like she's got a bone to pick with somebody," Finn said in a low voice.

"Let's get a better look," Sheila said, her heart racing with anticipation. She paused the video, zooming in on the girl's face as much as the low-quality footage allowed. Although the image was clearer than before, the face remained frustratingly indistinct.

"Damn," Sheila muttered under her breath, her gaze fixed on the blurred features of the potential suspect.

Finn's fingers drummed on the desk, a steady rhythm that filled the small room. He glanced at Sheila, his eyes narrowed in thought. "So we can't see her face," he said slowly, "but maybe there's another way to identify her."

"Like what?" Sheila asked, her focus still on the blurred image of the girl on the screen.

"Maybe we should go back to the college and show this picture to the faculty," Finn suggested. "Someone there might recognize her."

The idea made sense, but Sheila couldn't shake the feeling that there had to be a faster way to figure out who the girl was.

"Wait," she said suddenly, her voice hushed as if speaking louder might break the fragile thread of the idea forming in her mind. She leaned closer to the screen, studying the girl's movements again.

"There's something about the way she moves...it reminds me of someone I used to train with."

"Another kickboxer, you mean?"

"No," Sheila shook her head. "A wrestler." Her memories of the countless hours spent training in the gym played out like a film reel in her mind, her wrestler friend's distinct style etched into her mind. Whoever this girl on the security footage was, her movements were unmistakably those of a wrestler, purposeful and fluid, despite the grainy footage.

"It would make sense," Finn said, rubbing his chin.

"What do you mean?" Sheila asked.

"To get Kristen's body into that locker—it would take someone who can throw another's weight around. And who can do that better than a wrestler?"

CHAPTER TEN

The late afternoon sun cast long shadows across the nearly deserted campus, creating an eerie quiet that belied the anticipation hanging in the air. A gentle breeze rustled through the trees, scattering leaves onto the pathways as if nature itself were trying to conceal the true intentions of a predator.

Reagan leaned against a wall at the edge of the parking lot, waiting for Ami with the intensity of a hawk stalking its prey. The corners of Reagan's mouth curled into a sinister smile, baring teeth like a wolf in anticipation of the hunt. Obsession and determination burned in those cold eyes, fueled by a desire to punish Ami.

This was no mere whim or passing fancy; it was the culmination of countless hours spent brooding over Ami's transgressions. It was time for Ami to pay the price, and nothing would stand in the way of that singular goal.

Anticipation gnawed at Reagan, a tightening sensation in the chest that demanded resolution. Reagan wouldn't be denied any longer, not when vengeance was so close within reach.

"Where are you?" Reagan muttered, tension mounting with each passing second. And then, just like that, there she was—Ami's familiar blue sedan pulling into a parking space near the campus entrance.

"Gotcha," Reagan whispered.

As Ami stepped out of her car and locked the doors, Reagan waited a few moments, not wishing to ruin the plan by being too eager. Then, with calculated casualness, Reagan fell into step a few paces behind Ami, blending seamlessly into the sparse foot traffic.

Ami moved through the campus with an air of self-absorption, her attention glued to her phone screen. It seemed as though nothing else existed in her world, least of all the consequences of her actions.

"Typical," Reagan seethed internally, watching as Ami continued on her path without a care.

As if to prove the point, Ami collided with a young man who'd been walking in her direction. He stumbled slightly, looking up from his own phone in surprise.

"Hey, watch where you're going!" he said, irritation flashing across his face.

"Whatever," Ami muttered dismissively, not even bothering to look up from her screen as she brushed past him.

Reagan's anger, simmering up until this moment, began to boil at such callous indifference toward others. *Soon enough,* Reagan thought, *you'll realize how your decisions affect others.*

Reagan's breaths grew shallower with each step, keeping a careful eye on Ami as she continued to weave through the campus. Reagan's mind raced with thoughts of retribution, each scenario darker and more satisfying than the last.

Suddenly, Ami looked up from her phone, scanning the area around her. She took a sharp turn off the main path, opting for a shortcut through a smaller, more secluded park on campus.

Perfect, Reagan thought, smiling. *You're every bit as predictable as I'd hoped you'd be. Now, there will be no one to hear you scream.*

Ami strolled deeper into the park, still engrossed in her phone. The trees loomed overhead, their branches forming a canopy that filtered the fading sunlight, casting eerie patterns on the ground. Reagan's steps grew more purposeful, closing the distance with Ami, anticipation building with each stride.

Ami seemed completely unaware of the danger that stalked her, her every step taking her farther from the safety of the crowded campus and deeper into the secluded park. The muffled sounds of laughter and conversation vanished, replaced by the rhythmic chirping of crickets and the occasional distant car horn.

Thoughts of humiliation, betrayal, and countless sleepless nights spent plotting revenge swirled around in Reagan's mind like a tempest, driving Reagan forward with unwavering resolve.

Did she think she could get away with it? Does she even realize the depths of pain she's caused?

As Ami continued walking, still engrossed in her phone, Reagan took advantage of her distraction to move within striking distance. Reagan's heart pounded like a war drum, drowning out the soothing sounds of rustling leaves and the distant murmur of the nearby creek.

You're mine now, Reagan thought, fingers reaching into a pocket and fondling the knife concealed there. *All mine.*

CHAPTER ELEVEN

As Sheila pulled up a browser and entered the address of Coldwater Community College's official website, she rolled her shoulders, trying to shake off the fatigue accumulated from hours spent scouring the school's security footage.

Don't lose focus now, she told herself. *Not when you're so close.*

When the website appeared, she clicked on the athletics tab. A new page materialized, displaying various sports teams. After selecting the wrestling team, she noticed several things: a team photo, individual headshots, and a schedule of upcoming events.

"Okay, let's compare these faces with the one we have on the security footage," she said, her meticulous nature driving her to leave no stone unturned.

She pulled up the grainy image of the suspect on a separate window. The blurry face stared back at them, her features tantalizingly vague. Sheila then began the painstaking process of comparing each team member's face with the suspect's, scrutinizing every detail.

"She could be any of them," Finn said doubtfully. "There's simply not enough detail to go on."

Despite Finn's doubts and despite the limitations of the security footage, Sheila's keen eye for observation picked up on subtle similarities between their suspect and one of the wrestlers.

"Wait, look at this one," she said, pointing to a particular headshot. "There's something about her eyes and jawline that matches our suspect. I feel certain of it."

Finn squinted at the screen, his brow furrowing in concentration. "I suppose it's possible. Hard to be sure, though. But if you're confident..."

Sheila scrolled down the webpage, her heart pounding in anticipation. And there it was, the girl's name written in bold letters beneath her picture.

"Jade Larson," Sheila whispered, feeling her heart rate spike at the breakthrough. "We've got a name, Finn."

"Nice work, Sheila," Finn said, a proud smile tugging at the corners of his lips. "Now how do we find her?"

Sheila's fingers tapped eagerly on the keyboard as she searched for Jade Larson on various social media platforms. She found a Facebook profile first, and her eyes immediately scanned through the posts, looking for any relevant information.

"Looks like she's studying sports medicine," Sheila said. "And she's pretty active in the wrestling community."

"Anything that connects her to Kristen Lee?" Finn asked, his voice tense with anticipation.

As they scrolled further down Jade's timeline, Sheila noticed pictures of her participating in various wrestling events and hanging out with friends. Sheila's trained eye caught sight of a familiar face in one of the group photos.

"Wait, that's Lila Hartlett!" Finn said, pointing to the girl standing next to Jade, their arms wrapped around each other.

Sheila stared at Lila's familiar face. They had interviewed her just a few short hours ago. The question was, how well did these two know one another? Was it possible that this Jade Larson had gotten back at Kristen for hazing Lila? Was it possible Jade and Lila were in it together?

She began digging deeper, searching for any interactions between the two girls that might reveal more about their relationship. She soon discovered a series of public message threads between Jade and Lila that seemed to span months. Their conversations covered a wide range of topics, from discussing their shared love of sitcoms to venting about the stresses of college life.

"Look at this," Sheila said, pointing to one particular message. "It's from just a few hours ago. Lila mentions how grateful she is to have Jade in her life, especially after everything that happened with Kristen."

Finn leaned in closer, reading the messages alongside Sheila. It was clear from their exchanges that Jade and Lila had a close bond, supporting each other through both good times and bad.

"Seems like they're really good friends," Finn said, rubbing his chin thoughtfully. "Could Jade have taken things into her own hands to protect Lila from Kristen?"

"I was wondering the same thing myself."

"Maybe we should look into this Jade Larson, see if she's got a record."

Sheila's fingers flew over the keyboard as she accessed the police database.

"Here we go," she muttered under her breath, scanning the screen for any relevant information. She found a report filed by Kristen Lee a few months ago, accusing Jade of threatening her after a volleyball game. According to the report, Jade had cornered Kristen in the locker room and warned her to stay away from Lila. The report mentioned that an officer had spoken to Jade about the incident, but no further action was taken.

"Looks like Jade was pretty protective of Lila," Finn said as he read the report over Sheila's shoulder. "I'd say this gives her a solid motive."

Sheila nodded, her thoughts racing. If Jade was willing to threaten Kristen once, it was entirely possible that she would take things further.

"Wait a minute," she said suddenly, her eyes widening as she recalled a detail from earlier. "Remember when we were on the college's website? There was a wrestling event happening today." She navigated back to the site and clicked on the link for the wrestling team's schedule. Sure enough, there was an event listed for that afternoon. "This could be our chance to talk to Jade in person."

"Good catch," Finn said, his voice tense with anticipation. "Let's get over there before it ends, because if Jade sees us coming, there's no telling what she might do."

CHAPTER TWELVE

Sheila's breath misted in the chilly air as she and Finn walked toward Coldwater Community College's gymnasium, their footsteps echoing in the dimly lit pathway. The sun had dipped below the horizon, casting an eerie glow on the campus buildings. She felt a shiver run down her spine that had nothing to do with the cold.

"Can't believe they're still holding this wrestling tournament after what happened this morning," Sheila said, her voice tinged with disbelief as she and Finn walked toward Coldwater Community College's gymnasium. The sun had just dipped below the horizon, casting an eerie glow on the campus buildings.

Finn shrugged, his hands buried deep in the pockets of his jacket. "Life goes on, I guess. People need something to take their minds off tragedy."

Sheila couldn't argue with that, but it still didn't sit right. It made Kristen's death seem commonplace, trivial.

As they approached the gymnasium, the dull hum of chatter and the occasional cheer from within grew louder. The campus seemed to be holding its breath, the shadows cast by trees and lampposts stretching out like dark fingers across the grass.

Entering the gymnasium, the scent of sweat and adrenaline hit Sheila immediately. A cacophony of sounds assaulted her ears—sneakers squeaking on the polished floor, coaches barking orders, and the raucous noise of the crowd. It was strangely comforting; it reminded Sheila of her own years spent training and competing.

The gymnasium itself was a vast space with high ceilings and rows of bleacher seating filled with spectators. In the center, a spotlight illuminated the wrestling mat where two girls grappled fiercely. The tension in the room was palpable, as if everyone was clinging to this event as a way to forget, at least for a moment, the horrifying reality that lurked outside these walls.

Sheila scanned the faces in the crowd, searching for Jade Larson. She needed to talk to her about Kristen, but finding her in this sea of people would be no easy task.

"Come on," Finn said, nudging her gently. "Let's get closer and see what we see."

As they wove through the crowd, Sheila felt a sense of déjà vu, a longing for the days when she fought for glory and recognition. She missed the thrill of stepping into the ring, adrenaline pumping through her veins as she prepared to face an opponent. But those days were long gone, replaced by a different kind of fight—one that pitted her against the darkness lurking in Coldwater.

And tonight, that fight had led her to Jade Larson.

The atmosphere buzzed with excitement and energy as Sheila and Finn navigated through the mass of students. The metallic scent of sweat hung in the air, mingling with the aroma of buttery popcorn from a nearby concession stand.

"Where could she be?" Sheila muttered under her breath, craning her neck to catch a glimpse of Jade Larson. Her eyes darted between the two girls wrestling on the mat, their bodies taut with exertion, and the animated spectators surrounding them.

"Go, Hailey!" a woman shouted enthusiastically beside Sheila, startling her. The woman appeared to be in her forties, with short-cropped auburn hair and a face flushed with excitement. She wore a denim jacket adorned with various buttons. Sheila guessed she was cheering for her daughter.

"Excuse me," Sheila said, tapping the woman gently on the shoulder. "Do you know if Jade Larson is competing tonight?"

"Jade? Oh, I think she's up next," the woman replied, barely tearing her eyes away from the ongoing match. Then she raised her voice and shouted, "Keep your feet spread, Hailey! That's my girl!"

It was clear the woman was too focused on the match to give Sheila her full attention. Still, Sheila had one more question.

"Do you know where Jade is now?" she asked.

"Jade?" The woman sounded almost puzzled, as if she was so distracted that she didn't remember who they were talking about.

"Yes. Jade Larson?"

"She's probably in the next room, psyching herself up for the match. The tournament is almost over." She cupped her hands around her mouth and shouted, "Keep going, baby girl! You've got her right where you want her!"

"Thanks," Sheila said. Her gaze locked on the doorway of the next room, her thoughts racing. Had Jade seen them and decided to make a run for it? The uncertainty gnawed at her, but she knew she had to make a decision. Go after Jade, or wait for her to come out? She weighed the pros and cons in her mind, her heartbeat quickening with every passing second.

"What are the chances Jade saw us and took off?" Sheila asked Finn.

He frowned, his gaze growing thoughtful. "Let's give it another minute or two."

Sheila didn't particularly like this plan—if Jade had left, a minute or two could very well be the difference between catching her and letting her escape. Finn was the experienced one, however, and she trusted his judgment.

The wrestling match reached its climax as Hailey managed to pin her opponent to the ground. The referee blew his whistle, signaling the end of the match. Hailey caught her breath, her face flushed with victory, and retreated to the edge of the mat to speak with her trainer.

"Attention, everyone!" a voice boomed through the microphone, instantly quieting the chatter in the gymnasium. "We have reached the final match of the tournament. Please welcome back Hailey Robineaux and prepare for Jade Larson!"

Sheila's breathing grew shallow, and she felt the tension in the room rise with each passing moment as she waited to see whether Jade would emerge. The crowd held their breath collectively, their eyes fixed on the same doorway that had captivated her attention.

Seconds passed. Sheila shifted her weight from one foot to the other. Finally, she turned to Finn. "You sure she's gonna show?" she asked.

In answer, Finn pointed. Sheila turned and watched as the door to the gymnasium swung open, and Jade Larson strode into the room. She was a stocky, athletic girl with tightly braided dark hair and a fierce expression set on her face. Her opponent, Hailey Robineaux, was equally muscular, but there was something softer about her features as she waited for Jade to enter the ring.

"Here we go," Sheila murmured under her breath as the two wrestlers faced off in the center of the mat.

"I have to make a confession," Finn said, raising his voice to be heard above the excited crowd.

"What's that?" Sheila asked.

"I really don't know anything about wrestling—not as a sport, I mean. What's it all about?"

"Well," Sheila said, stepping closer to Finn as they watched the match unfold. "Wrestling is about control. It's a physical and mental battle to dominate your opponent and pin them down. To be successful, you need strength, agility, balance, and technique. But you also need to be able to read your opponent, anticipate their moves, and react quickly. It's all about outsmarting and overpowering your opponent."

"Kind of like kickboxing?"

"Similar, but also different," Sheila replied. "In kickboxing, you're trying to knock your opponent out or score points by hitting certain areas of their body. In wrestling, you're trying to control your opponent's body and pin them down for a certain amount of time. It's a more intimate form of combat, in a way."

Finn nodded, his eyes glued to the match.

Jade and Sarah circled each other warily, sizing up their opponent before lunging in to engage. Their movements were fluid and precise as they grappled, each one seeking an advantage over the other. Sheila noticed that Jade's style was particularly aggressive, her muscles tensing as she fought to dominate the match.

"Look at Jade," she said to Finn. "See how she's using her anger to fuel her performance? It's making her unpredictable, which can be both an asset and a liability in a match like this."

Finn nodded, watching intently as Jade managed to take Hailey down with a swift maneuver. It was clear that Jade's rage gave her an edge, but it also seemed to be taking a toll on her. As the match continued, Jade's face grew increasingly flushed and her breathing became more labored.

"Is that normal?" Finn asked, concern evident in his voice as he gestured toward Jade.

Sheila pursed her lips, considering the situation. "It's not uncommon for a wrestler to get worked up during a match, but Jade's anger seems… excessive. It's almost as if she's fighting something other than just Hailey."

The tension in the gymnasium thickened as Jade and Sarah continued their battle on the wrestling mat. Their muscles strained, limbs entwined, as they fought for control. Finn leaned in closer to Sheila, his eyes locked on the match.

"You miss it?" Finn asked. "Kickboxing? Or does police work scratch that itch?"

"Both, in a way," she said. "I miss kickboxing, the rush of it, the adrenaline. But I also love what I do now, the sense of purpose it gives me. And it's not like I can't still train and spar, you know?"

As the match wore on, Jade managed to gain the upper hand. She wrapped her arms around Hailey's waist and executed a powerful takedown, sending her opponent crashing to the mat. The crowd gasped as Jade swiftly transitioned into a pinning position, her legs hooked around Hailey's thighs to immobilize her.

"Jade's got her now," Sheila murmured, her heart pounding in anticipation. "She just needs to hold this position for the count."

The referee hovered nearby, his hand poised to slap the mat as he counted down the seconds. Jade's face was a portrait of raw intensity, her eyes fierce and unyielding as she kept Hailey pinned.

"That's it!" the referee said. "We have our winner!"

Despite this declaration, however, Jade maintained her iron grip on Hailey for a few tense seconds. Then she let go, pushing the other girl away as she rose.

She didn't want to let go, Sheila thought. *She wanted to hurt her.*

"Wow," Finn said, clearly impressed by Jade's performance. "That was intense."

"Definitely," Sheila said as the crowd clapped. "She gave it everything she had."

As Hailey struggled to stand, she offered Jade a congratulatory handshake. However, Jade merely glanced at the gesture, her expression cold and aloof, before turning away. The crowd applauded as Jade was presented with a gleaming trophy, a testament to her hard-won victory.

"Come on," Sheila said to Finn, her gaze fixed on Jade. "Let's see if we can catch her before she leaves."

They maneuvered through the throng of spectators, keeping their eyes on Jade as she posed for pictures with her family. Sheila could sense the pride radiating from Jade's relatives, but couldn't help noticing the tightness around Jade's eyes, as if she was holding back some deeper emotion.

Before Sheila and Finn could get any closer, Jade, still glistening with sweat from her match, left the gymnasium and disappeared down a hallway. Sheila and Finn followed closely behind through the near-empty corridor. They passed several closed doors before finally catching a glimpse of Jade entering the pool room.

As they stepped inside, Sheila was met by a wave of humid air, along with the sharp scent of chlorine. The large Olympic-sized pool seemed to dominate the space, its water reflecting the dim lights overhead, casting rippling shadows on the tiled walls. Rows of empty bleachers lined one side of the room while the other hosted various pieces of swim training equipment. The sound of a faint drip echoed through the otherwise silent room.

"Jade!" Sheila said, catching the attention of the young wrestler as she headed toward the showers.

Jade turned around, her eyes narrowed slightly. "What do you want?" she asked. "I need to get cleaned up."

Sheila stepped forward, watching the wrestler carefully. Finn was on her left, standing at the edge of the pool that shimmered gently, blue as the sky on a summer's day.

"We need to talk to you about Kristen Lee," Sheila said.

The mention of Kristen's name seemed to strike a chord within Jade. Her expression flickered with anger and uncertainty, but it was quickly replaced by a hard mask of determination. She glanced back at the shower entrance, her fingers clenching and unclenching.

"Why do you want to talk about Kristen?" she demanded, her voice tight with suspicion. Her eyes were dark pools of emotion, wavering between anger and fear.

Finn shifted his weight from one foot to the other, a hint of uncertainty. "We heard that you threatened her," he said, choosing his words carefully. "Is that true?"

Jade hesitated for a moment, her eyes flicking back and forth between Finn and Sheila. The silence stretched on, the question hanging heavy in the air.

"Did you threaten Kristen, Jade?" Sheila pressed gently, trying to keep her tone non-confrontational. But despite her best efforts, she could feel her own frustration bubbling beneath the surface, fueled by the urgency of their investigation.

Jade walked toward Sheila, her eyes hard. Everything about her posture screamed to Sheila that the girl was on the edge, ready to attack at a moment's notice. Sheila resisted the urge to shift into a fighting stance, instead behaving as casually as she could manage.

"What did you just say?" Jade asked in a low voice.

"It's just a question," Finn said. "Why don't you come down to the station with us, and—"

Before Finn could finish, Jade turned and gave him a two-handed shove. Caught off guard, Finn stumbled backward, his arms windmilling in a futile attempt to regain his balance. He hit the water with a resounding splash, sending droplets spraying into the air.

And then Jade ran.

CHAPTER THIRTEEN

Sheila's heart pounded in her chest as she sprinted through the dimly lit halls of Coldwater Community College, her breaths ragged and heavy. The sound of Jade Larson's retreating footsteps fueled Sheila's determination to catch up with her. She could see Jade's muscular form weaving around corners, a blur in the darkness.

"Jade, stop!" Sheila shouted, but Jade only increased her pace, surprisingly quick giving her stocky build.

As Sheila rounded another corner, she spotted Jade disappearing into a large room down the hall. Upon entering the room, Sheila found herself surrounded by solemn faces. Students gathered in clusters, their eyes red-rimmed and filled with grief. The air vibrated with the hushed tones of whispered conversations.

The room was awash in soft candlelight, casting shadows against the walls, which were adorned with photos of Kristen. Her bright smile seemed so full of life, making it hard to believe she was gone. Posters and banners displayed messages of love and remembrance, and a table near the entrance was strewn with flowers, handwritten notes, and mementos.

Sheila's heart pounded in her chest, sweat beading on her forehead as she scanned the crowd for any sign of Jade. The room buzzed with quiet conversations, whispers of grief and loss floating through the air like a somber melody. Her eyes locked onto a figure near the back, slipping through a door just as it began to close.

"Jade!" Sheila called, ignoring the frowning faces that turned toward her. She pushed through the sea of mourners, fighting her way to the far side of the room.

As she reached the door through which Jade had disappeared, she hesitated only a moment before yanking it open and stepping into the dimly lit hallway. She peered into the darkness, catching a glimpse of Jade's form disappearing around another corner.

"Stop, Jade! I just want to talk!" Sheila shouted, her voice echoing through the empty corridor as she sprinted after the fleeing suspect.

Her lungs burned, her breath coming in ragged gasps as she rounded the corner. A large exercise room loomed ahead, filled with rows of treadmills, stationary bikes, and weightlifting equipment. The walls were lined with mirrors, reflecting the fluorescent lights that flickered overhead.

"Damn it," she muttered under her breath, her eyes darting around the room for any sign of Jade. The once pristine gym now felt like a maze, a labyrinth of machines and shadows that could hide her quarry all too well.

"Where are you?" Sheila whispered to herself, scanning the room with determination. She knew Jade couldn't have gone far, but every second that ticked by felt like an eternity. If Jade had already left the room, then every second Sheila spent here would only allow Jade to increase her lead.

She took a few tentative steps forward, navigating the maze of equipment as she searched for the elusive wrestler. "I just want to talk, Jade. That's all."

The scent of sweat and disinfectant permeated the air, a familiar aroma that normally brought her comfort but now only heightened her unease. The whir of the air conditioning above was the only sound that accompanied her footsteps, the silence otherwise oppressive.

"Please," she continued, her voice strained with desperation. "I'm not here to hurt you."

A flicker of movement in one of the mirrors caught her eye, and she spun around just in time to see Jade lunging at her. Sheila's instincts kicked in, and she raised her arms to block the powerful blow aimed at her face. Jade's solid frame collided with hers, the impact reverberating through Sheila's body.

"Get off me!" Sheila said, pushing Jade back with all her strength. The wrestler snarled, determined to pin Sheila to the ground, her muscles straining against Sheila's resistance. Sheila knew she needed distance—the close proximity favored Jade's grappling expertise.

A swift kick to Jade's midsection sent her stumbling backward, buying Sheila the space she desperately needed. A moment later, however, Jade was lunging toward her again, her face twisted with rage.

Sheila deflected her attack with a well-timed side-step, then retaliated with a series of quick jabs and kicks, each one expertly aimed to keep Jade at bay.

"Enough!" Sheila said, trying to establish control of the situation. "I don't want to hurt you, but I will if I have to!"

As their eyes locked, something shifted in Jade's gaze—a flicker of uncertainty, perhaps even vulnerability. But just as quickly, it vanished, replaced once more by the steely determination that defined her. Her hands clenched into fists, her eyes darting around the room for an advantage. Her gaze locked onto a dumbbell resting on the floor nearby.

"Jade, don't!" Sheila warned, recognizing the danger in her opponent's eyes. But it was already too late. Jade lunged for the dumbbell, gripping it tightly in her hand before swinging it at Sheila with all her might.

Sheila, acting entirely on instinct, jerked her body to the side. The dumbbell whizzed past her, missing her head by mere inches as it flew from Jade's hand. Jade had over-committed, the heavyweight dragging her body forward, and Sheila took advantage of the opportunity. Grasping Jade's arm, she twisted it behind her back, immobilizing her. Jade grunted in pain, but Sheila held firm.

"Let me go!" Jade demanded, her voice dark with fury. She tried to wriggle from Sheila's grasp, but Sheila clung to her, knowing that if she allowed Jade to escape, this fight could turn around in a hurry.

"Okay," Jade said softly. "I surrender. Just, please—my arm's really hurting."

Sheila relaxed her hold just a little. In the same moment, Jade jerked her arm free, twisting away. Sheila was ready for just such an attempt, however. Anticipating Jade's move, she tripped the wrestler, sending her sprawling to the ground. Before Jade could recover, Sheila knelt on her back, pinning her down with practiced ease.

"Jade Larson, you're under arrest," she said, her breath coming in ragged gasps as she snapped the handcuffs around the other woman's wrists.

Just then, the door to the exercise room burst open, and Finn Mercer stumbled in, water dripping from his hair and clothes. His soaked jacket clung to his body, making him look like a drowned rat–but a determined one.

"Sheils, are you alright?" he asked, his eyes scanning the room, taking in the sight of Jade pinned beneath Sheila.

"Oh, just peachy," she said, her muscles straining to keep Jade restrained. Despite her apparent fear moments earlier, Jade's anger had reignited, fueling her renewed attempts to break free.

Sheila pulled Jade to her feet. "Let's get to the station," she said. "We've got some questions to ask you about Kristen Lee."

"Kristen?" Jade laughed bitterly. "She deserved what she got, and if you think I'm going to feel sorry for her for one second, then you can think again!"

CHAPTER FOURTEEN

Sheila was still mulling over Jade's words about Kristen getting what she deserved when Finn stepped out of the sheriff's department locker room. She couldn't help but notice how sharp he looked in his borrowed uniform. The night sky outside cast a silvery glow through the narrow windows, accentuating the creases and lines of the crisp, navy blue fabric.

"Sorry about the wait," Finn said, adjusting the collar of his uniform. "Had to borrow this one from a friend since mine got soaked."

"It looks good on you," Sheila said, offering him an encouraging smile.

Finn grunted. "A little tight around the armpits, but it'll do. Come on, we shouldn't leave Jade waiting."

The sheriff's department was alive with activity despite the late hour; officers hurried past them, carrying stacks of paperwork and discussing cases in hushed tones. The harsh fluorescent lights flickered overhead, casting a sterile glow on the beige walls lined with wanted posters and community event flyers.

Sheila's ears perked up as she overheard two deputies talking nearby. One deputy, a middle-aged man with graying hair, leaned against a desk while the other, a younger woman with short-cropped blonde hair, flipped through a file.

"Did you hear about that case down in Millersville?" the older deputy asked, his voice low and somber. "The one where they found the body of that real estate agent in the trunk of her own car?"

"Yeah, I heard," the younger deputy replied, shaking her head. "Poor woman. It sounds like she was just in the wrong place at the wrong time. They think it might have been a serial killer passing through town."

"Damn shame," the older deputy muttered, rubbing his temples. "We've got enough on our plates without worrying about serial killers."

Sheila shivered involuntarily, her thoughts drifting back to Jade and the mystery that surrounded her. She wondered whether Jade was capable of hiding something as dark and sinister as murder. As they approached the interview room door, she steeled herself for the confrontation that lay ahead and hoped she could uncover the truth.

At the door, Finn paused and turned to her. "I want you to take the lead on this one," he said, his eyes serious.

"Are you sure?" she asked, surprised by his sudden decision. Even though she had taken the lead most of the day, she'd never done so with an official police interview.

"Absolutely," Finn said with a slight nod. "You may be inexperienced, and you still have a lot to prove, but you've shown me a lot in the short time we've worked together." He placed a reassuring hand on her shoulder. "I'll be right there to back you up as needed."

Sheila took a deep breath, feeling a flutter in her stomach at her new responsibility. With a determined nod, she followed Finn into the interview room.

The room was small, its bare walls painted a pale blue. A single overhead light cast stark shadows across the floor and table. At the far end of the room sat Jade Larson, her stocky, athletic frame slouched in a chair. She was cuffed to the table, her dark hair falling in messy strands around her face. Her eyes met theirs, narrowing into a glare as silence hung heavy in the air.

Sheila cleared her throat as she sat down across from Jade Larson, her heart pounding. The stark fluorescent lights overhead cast an unforgiving glare on the metal table separating them. She could feel Finn's presence beside her, a silent pillar of support.

"Let's start with the basics," she said, her voice steady despite the fluttering in her stomach. "Please confirm your name for the record."

"Jade Larson," came the grudging reply, Jade's dark eyes narrowing as she met Sheila's gaze.

"Thank you," Sheila said, folding her hands on the table. "Now, Jade, can you tell us why you ran?"

"Look, I didn't have anything to do with Kristen Lee's murder," Jade said, her voice tense and defensive. "I just...I didn't like her, okay? What she did to Lila was nothing short of barbaric, but that doesn't mean I'd kill her or anything."

Sheila recalled watching Jade's last wrestling match and how ferocious she had seemed, like a caged animal unleashed upon her opponents. "We watched your last match," she said. "You looked angry, like you really wanted to hurt your opponents. Where do you think that anger comes from?"

"Blowing off steam, that's all," Jade said, looking away. "School can be stressful, you know?"

Sheila pursed her lips, her eyes searching Jade's face for any sign of deception. It was true that school could be overwhelming, but something about Jade's explanation felt incomplete. Were those clenched fists at her side merely a reaction to stress, or was there something darker lurking beneath?

The tension in the room seemed to ebb for a moment, and Jade's shoulders relaxed ever so slightly. Her eyes flicked to her wrists, still cuffed to the table, and she swallowed hard before speaking up. "So, what's going to happen to me now? Are you going to put me in jail for fighting you guys?"

Finn arched an eyebrow, his surprise evident. "Jail? Jade, we're trying to figure out if you were involved in Kristen Lee's murder, not whether you threw a few punches at us." His voice was calm but firm, as if he couldn't believe that Jade's priorities lay elsewhere.

Sheila's gaze locked on Jade's face. She could sense the barely contained panic behind the wrestler's eyes, and it dawned on her what truly mattered to Jade.

"I know you're worried about your wrestling career," Sheila said. "You don't want anyone to find out that you fought with us, because it could lead to you being expelled from the team, right?"

Jade's jaw tightened, and she looked away, unable to meet Sheila's knowing gaze. It was clear that Sheila had struck a nerve, and Jade's silence spoke volumes. Sheila leaned in closer, placing her hands on the table, her voice soft yet unwavering.

"Here's the deal, Jade. If you don't come clean with us, we'll have no choice but to book you for assault. The college will need to know about it, and there's a good chance you'll be disciplined or even dismissed by your wrestling team. Is that really a risk you're willing to take?"

A shudder ran through Jade's body, and Sheila could see the internal struggle playing out on her face. She knew that wrestling meant everything to this young woman, and the thought of losing it must have been absolutely terrifying. But Sheila also knew that this was their best chance at getting to the truth.

Jade's eyes filled with tears as she clasped her cuffed hands together, her knuckles turning white with the force of her grip. "Please," she implored Sheila, her voice trembling, "don't do this to me.

Wrestling is my life. It's the only thing that makes me feel like I'm worth something."

Sheila watched as the girl before her seemed to crumble under an invisible weight. She couldn't help but feel a pang of sympathy for Jade, remembering her own days as a competitive athlete.

"Jade," Sheila said softly, leaning in closer, "I understand how important wrestling is to you. But we need to know the truth. If you cooperate and tell us everything, we'll do our best to help you."

Jade bit her lip, struggling to hold back her tears. "Wrestling is really the only thing I enjoy," she said, her voice cracking. "I suck at school, and things aren't great with my family at home, either. When I get in the ring—that's the only time I feel like I'm in control of something. If I lose that..."

"If you cooperate fully with us," Sheila said, "we won't press charges. I can't guarantee that nobody saw us leading you out of the school in handcuffs, but we'll do what we can on our end to prevent this from having any negative impact on your career."

For a moment, it seemed as if Jade might refuse, but then she let out a shuddering breath, dropping her gaze to the table. "Fine," she muttered, defeated. "What do you want to know?"

"Tell us about Kristen," Sheila said, sensing they were finally getting somewhere. "Did you ever confront her about the incident with Lila?"

Jade nodded. "I said some things, gave her a piece of my mind. I was just so angry for Lila's sake, and I wanted Kristen to know how it felt to be scared."

"That's all you did?" Finn asked. "You just talked to her?"

"That's all."

"And when did this conversation take place?"

"A few weeks ago. I don't remember when."

"Then why were you pacing in front of her room last night?"

Jade's eyes widened. "How did you know about that?"

"Just answer the question," Sheila said.

"I..." Jade swallowed hard. "I'd just seen Lila – she only just came back to school after resting at home for *months* – and the way she was limping around—it just pissed me off, made everything feel like it had just happened again."

"So you went to Kristen's room to confront her," Sheila said.

"Yes, but I didn't actually see her. I thought better of it and left. I swear."

"And where'd you go after that?" Finn asked, studying her carefully.

"Please, you have to believe me," Jade pleaded, her voice cracking under the weight of her desperation. "I went to a friend's room. We had a group project due, and we were up late working on it. There were four of us: me, Lila, and two other teammates, Becca and Sarah. You can ask them, they'll tell you I was there."

Sheila felt the tension in the room ease as Jade provided her alibi, and she found herself believing the girl's words. She glanced over at Finn, who seemed to be weighing the information as well.

"Look, I know I messed up by fighting you guys, and I swear I'm sorry for that, but I didn't kill Kristen," Jade insisted, her gaze darting between Sheila and Finn. "You have to believe me."

There was one question still left unanswered. "If that's really the case," Sheila said, "then why did you run when you saw us? Why did you fight so hard to keep us from questioning you?"

"Don't lie to us," Finn warned. "It will only make things more difficult for you."

Jade glanced from Sheila to Finn, then back again, her eyes shining with desperation. She looked trapped, as if her mind were racing for some solution to get her out of the predicament she was in.

Finally, she sighed and lowered her gaze to the floor. "I thought you were here about the EpiPens," she said softly.

Sheila and Finn exchanged a puzzled glance. "EpiPens?" Sheila asked.

Jade nodded. "I got injured a while back – pulled a hamstring – and even after recovering, I realized I'd lost a step. I couldn't bear to lose…so I faked a re-injury, and while I was at the infirmary, I swiped some Epi-Pens."

It all made sense to Sheila now. Jade had been high on adrenaline when they confronted her, which, combined with her desire to protect a secret that would have gotten her disqualified from the sport she loved so much, had led her to respond on instinct, running and then fighting back for all she was worth.

Sheila sat back in her chair, the metal legs scraping against the floor as she did so. Her mind raced, trying to process the information Jade had given them. If Jade wasn't responsible for Kristen's murder, who was?

Just as Sheila was about to speak, her phone vibrated in her pocket. She pulled it out and saw Natalie's name displayed on the screen. With a quick glance at Finn, who gave her a nod of understanding, she stood up.

"Wait," Jade said suddenly. "What's going to happen now? You're not going to share what I said, are you?"

"I'd rather leave that to you." Sheila placed a hand on the younger woman's shoulder. "Whatever competitive edge you think the adrenaline has been giving you, it isn't worth the weight of secrecy and shame. The best thing you can do now is tell the truth and leave the rest in the school's hands."

"But what if they kick me out? What if they never let me wrestle again?" Her eyes shone with tears.

"Sometimes you just have to do the right thing, regardless of the consequences," Sheila said gently. "You'll feel better once you do."

Jade swallowed hard and nodded, pressing her lips together bravely. Giving the wrestler's shoulder a parting squeeze, Sheila left the interview room to return her sister's call.

"Hey, Nat," Sheila said into the phone, her voice hushed as she stepped out into the busy hallway of the sheriff's department. "What's up?"

"How's the investigation going?" Natalie asked, cutting straight to the point.

Sheila leaned against the cool wall, her eyes scanning the bustling office as deputies hurried back and forth with files and coffee cups in hand. She hesitated for a moment before giving Natalie a brief summary of their interview with Jade. "We just brought in a wrestler, Jade Larson, who had motive to harm Kristen," she said. "It seems unlikely at this point she's involved, but we'll have to look into her alibi to be sure."

Natalie sighed on the other end of the line, her concern evident even over the phone. "That's not going to be necessary."

Sheila frowned. "Why not?"

"Because another body was just found at Clearview University. And from what I've been told, the victim probably hasn't been dead more than an hour or two—which means the killer could still be close by."

CHAPTER FIFTEEN

Sheila's heart raced as she gripped the steering wheel, Finn beside her in the passenger seat as they drove to Clearview University. The night seemed to close in around them, suffocating and heavy with the scent of fear.

Natalie's words echoed in Sheila's mind: *The victim probably hasn't been dead more than an hour or two—which means the killer could still be close by.*

As they entered the campus of Clearview University, Sheila's eyes darted between the buildings and the students milling about. The campus was a mix of old brick structures and modern glass edifices, bathed in the harsh glow of fluorescent streetlights. In the midst of this architectural dance, the students seemed like shadows flitting between realities.

"Look at them," she said softly, her thoughts slipping through her lips as she studied the young faces passing by. "Do you think one of them could be the killer?"

Finn glanced out the window, his face a mask of grim determination. "Right now, we can't rule anything out. But there's not much point in guessing, not unless you spot someone holding a bloody knife."

Sheila swallowed hard, her throat dry, and tried to ignore the churning in her stomach. She knew this was part of the job, but she had never visited a murder scene before, not while the body was still there. Every fiber of her being screamed for her to turn back, to flee from the horrors lurking just out of sight. But she knew she couldn't. She wouldn't.

She parked their car in front of the Nelson Science Building, a modern structure with sleek lines and large windows. The area was already swarming with police cruisers, their red and blue lights casting eerie shadows across the pavement. A tall, muscular officer stood guard at the entrance, his face marred by a grimace as he glanced toward the building's interior.

"Hey, Officer Kwan," Finn said. "How bad is it inside?"

"Pretty bad, Mercer," the officer replied, his voice heavy with dread. "You'll see for yourself soon enough."

Sheila swallowed hard, her stomach twisting into anxious knots. The thought of what awaited her behind those doors sent shivers down her spine.

As Sheila and Finn entered the building, they were met by the sterile scent of disinfectant and the low hum of fluorescent lights overhead. The once-spotless linoleum floors were now marred by muddy footprints and the hurried scuffs of countless law enforcement boots.

"Sounds like they're this way," Finn said, nodding toward the faint voices drifting toward them from down the hall. They followed the sound, the tension between them palpable as they ventured deeper into the building.

The hallway lined with lockers was a chaotic tableau. Police officers huddled together, exchanging information in hushed tones while a few teachers stood off to the side, their faces pale and stricken. The janitor leaned against a wall, wringing his mop in his hands as if trying to cleanse himself of the horror he'd witnessed.

In the center of it all, an open locker yawned wide, revealing a gruesome sight within. Though Sheila couldn't see the body itself, blocked as it was by a police officer crouching to take photographs, she could see the dark crimson pool of blood spreading across the floor.

Her heart sank at the sight, and she fought to keep her emotions in check. The air felt thick with fear, and for the first time in her life, Sheila found herself questioning her ability to face what lay ahead.

The officer taking pictures finally stepped aside, and Sheila's breath caught in her throat as she saw the body. The victim was a young college girl, her fit frame sprawled lifelessly on the cold floor. Her once vibrant eyes were now glazed over, staring blankly at the ceiling. Her blouse was slashed and soaked with blood from the multiple stab wounds that marred her body. A crimson halo framed her head, giving an eerie contrast to her golden hair.

Sheila's stomach churned, and bile rose in her throat as she stared at the gruesome sight before her. She had never seen anything so brutal, so heart-wrenching. Tears pricked at the corners of her eyes, and she turned away, unable to look at the mangled corpse any longer.

"Hey," Finn said softly, wrapping his arms around her and pulling her into a comforting hug. "I know it's tough, but you're strong, Sheila. We'll find this monster."

Sheila nodded against Finn's chest, trying to steady her breathing and regain control. As they stood there, Natalie approached them, her wheelchair making almost no noise on the linoleum floor. With a heavy, grave expression on her face, she looked at Sheila.

"I know it's horrible," she said. "I've seen my fair share of murder victims over the years, but this one…this one is particularly bad. The killer is vicious, heartless. Are you going to be okay, Sheila?"

Sheila disentangled herself from Finn's embrace and wiped her eyes, feeling a mixture of gratitude and discomfort toward her sister. She took a deep breath, willing herself to focus on the task at hand.

"I—I'll be fine," she stammered, her voice wavering slightly. "What do we know about the victim?"

"Her name was Ami Nasir," Natalie began, her voice steady despite the grim scene around them. "She was a sophomore here at Clearview, majoring in nutrition. A star athlete on the basketball team. Well-liked by her peers, at least as far as we can tell."

Sheila listened intently, trying to piece together any possible connections that could lead them to the killer. As they stood there, an elderly woman slowly approached them, her white hair neatly pinned back and her eyes clouded with concern. She wore a simple, long dress that appeared to have been worn countless times, yet still maintained an air of elegance.

"Excuse me," she said softly, drawing their attention. "I'm Mrs. Fairbanks, the history teacher here at Clearview. We're all just devastated by Ami's death. She was always such a good student, polite and respectful in class. She never caused any problems."

The woman paused, biting her lip as if hesitant to continue. "Of course, there were rumors about her being hard on some of the other basketball players in practice, but I always thought they were just that—rumors. Do you have any idea who could've done this?"

Natalie offered Mrs. Fairbanks a sympathetic smile. "Thank you for sharing your thoughts with us, ma'am. We're doing everything we can to find the person responsible. If you wouldn't mind, Officer Daniels over there would be more than happy to take your statement and any additional information you might have."

Nodding gratefully, Mrs. Fairbanks shuffled over to the young police officer standing nearby. He greeted her warmly, offering a comforting hand on her shoulder as she began to recount her memories of Ami to him.

As Sheila watched Mrs. Fairbanks walk away, her mind churned with possibilities. The dimly lit hallway cast shadows on the faces of everyone present, making their expressions hard to read. The scent of antiseptic and the metallic tang of blood filled her nostrils, a sickening reminder of the gruesome scene before her.

"Hey," Finn said, studying her with concern in his eyes. "You sure you're alright?"

Sheila forced a smile and nodded, brushing a strand of hair from her face. "Yeah, I'm just thinking about what Mrs. Fairbanks said...about Ami being hard on other students."

Natalie frowned thoughtfully. "What are you getting at?"

"Maybe someone killed her out of jealousy," Sheila said. "Ami was a star athlete, after all. And if the rumors are true..." She paused. "Maybe she pushed someone too far."

CHAPTER SIXTEEN

Sheila's eyes ached as they darted across the dimly lit table, which was strewn with school files on the three victims. Desperate to find that single thread linking all three crimes, she furrowed her brow, the weight of her exhaustion settling in like a heavy fog. The fluorescent lights above buzzed softly, casting an eerie glow over the late-night scene. *What am I missing?* she thought desperately.

The cafeteria at Clearview University was deserted, save for Sheila, Natalie, and Finn. Long shadows stretched across the empty space. The table was strewn with the remnants of their takeout food: greasy cartons and crumpled napkins scattered haphazardly around the school files. The scent of stale coffee mingled with the faint aroma of cleaning supplies.

Sheila rubbed her tired eyes, the strain of staring at the files for hours taking its toll. She glanced over at Natalie and Finn, both of them hunched over their respective documents with furrowed brows. The dimly lit cafeteria felt more like a temporary bunker than a place where students normally gathered to eat and socialize. The only sounds were the distant hum of the air conditioning unit and the faint, rhythmic tapping of a leaky faucet.

"Are you sure these are all the files?" she asked Finn.

Finn lifted his gaze from the papers, dark bags underlining his eyes. "Yes, I spoke with the presidents of all three colleges. They know how important this is."

Sheila drummed her fingers on the table, the frustration welling inside her. "What if there were incidents where the victims bullied someone, but they weren't recorded?"

Natalie considered the suggestion, her eyes narrowing in thought. "That's possible, but how would we find out about those incidents? It's not like bullies keep a record of their actions."

"Maybe we could talk to the victims' friends and families," Finn said, rolling his shoulders to ease tension. "Find out if anyone was harboring resentment toward them."

Natalie shook her head, her expression grim. "That'll take too long. The killer has struck twice within twenty-four hours. We don't have time to waste."

As silence descended upon the group once more, Sheila's mind raced with possibilities, each one running into frustrating dead-ends. They needed answers, but the clues remained elusive. She clenched her fists beneath the table, the ache in her knuckles mirroring the growing desperation she felt. Time was slipping away, and with it, any hope of preventing another senseless death.

Feeling the weight of time bearing down on them, she pulled out her phone to check the hour. The glowing screen read ten o'clock, the numbers taunting her with their unwavering march forward.

An unread message from her father caught her eye: *How's Natalie? Does she seem normal to you?*

That was strange. Did Dad know something about Natalie that Sheila didn't?

Swallowing hard, she looked up at Natalie and Finn, their focus still locked on the investigation.

"Hey, I...I need a breather," she said. "I'm going to walk around, clear my head. I'll be back shortly."

Natalie glanced up, concern etched on her face. "You okay?"

"Fine. Just need some fresh air." She forced a smile, trying to reassure her sister.

Rising, Sheila strode out of the room, entered a hallway, and followed it all the way to the exit. As she stepped outside into the crisp night air, leaving the oppressive ambiance of the cafeteria behind, the Clearview University campus spread before her like an oasis of knowledge, its well-manicured lawns and modern architecture bathed in the soft glow of streetlights. Shadows danced across the empty pathways as leaves rustled in the gentle breeze, the silence of the night occasionally broken by distant laughter or footsteps echoing through the darkness.

Despite the tranquil exterior, a palpable tension hung over the campus. Police cars prowled along the perimeter, their presence a somber reminder of the danger lurking within. It was as if the entire university held its breath, waiting for the next strike.

As she walked, Sheila's thoughts drifted to Natalie. Her sister had always been the stronger one, the golden child, but now she found herself confined to a wheelchair and facing an uncertain future. Sheila wondered how much of Natalie's stubborn determination was a mask, hiding her own fear and vulnerability.

Pausing in the shadows, she leaned against a brick wall and pulled out her phone. She hesitated for a moment before calling her father. As it rang, she glanced around at the darkened campus, feeling a shiver run down her spine that had nothing to do with the cold.

"Hey, Sheila," he said with a tired sigh. "How's my little girl?"

"Not so little any more. I hope I'm not interrupting anything."

"Ah, Sheila," Gabe replied warmly. "No, you're not interrupting. I was just painting, but my eyes were getting blurry and I was about to wrap up for the night anyway."

"Painting?" Sheila couldn't help but smile at the thought of her father – who had been both a hardnosed kickboxer and no-nonsense law enforcement officer in his time – wielding a paintbrush instead of a pistol or boxing gloves. It seemed so unlike him, and yet, she was glad he had found a creative outlet in his twilight years.

"Really? What are you painting?" she asked, genuinely curious.

"Actually, it's a landscape of Coldwater," Gabe said, his voice taking on a wistful tone. "You know, the view from our backyard, overlooking the Great Salt Lake. I thought it would be a nice reminder of home for you girls."

Sheila felt a warmth spreading through her chest as she pictured her dad carefully capturing the rugged beauty of their hometown. It was endearing, this softer side of him, and she cherished these rare glimpses into his heart.

"Wow, Dad, that sounds amazing," she murmured. "I can't wait to see it."

"Me neither." Gabe chuckled. "I'm not much of an artist, but it's been a good way to relax, you know?"

"Definitely," Sheila said, her gaze drifting across the eerily quiet campus once more. She wished she could share her father's sense of peace, but the weight of the unsolved case pressed down on her like a leaden blanket.

The silence lingered for a moment, heavy with unspoken thoughts. Sheila could almost hear the brushstrokes of her father's painting. Finally, Gabe cleared his throat.

"How's Natalie doing?" he asked. "You seen her much lately?"

Sheila sighed, her gaze falling onto the dark pavement beneath her feet. "A bit. I don't really know how she's doing, Dad. She keeps things close to her chest, doesn't open up much—at least not to me."

"Ah, yes," Gabe murmured, understanding in his tone. "She's always been like that. It's hard for her to show vulnerability."

"Especially now," Sheila added, thinking about her sister's injury and the wheelchair that had become such an unwelcome part of her life. "She seems to be coping, but I can tell it's difficult for her."

Gabe's voice grew somber. "It's a tough adjustment, no doubt about it. But your sister's strong. She'll find her way through this."

"I just wish there was more I could do to help," Sheila said, frustration bubbling up inside her.

"So do I, Sheila. So do I." His voice had grown thoughtful, almost sad. Then he took a quick breath, signaling a change in topic. "So, how are you liking police work?"

"Mostly it's been good," she replied, hesitating for a moment before adding, "but seeing my first body…that was tough."

"Ah, I remember my first one," Gabe said, his voice both somber and nostalgic. "It was a hit-and-run, out on the highway. The poor guy was barely recognizable. I was just a rookie, and it shook me to my core."

Sheila could almost picture her father standing there, a young officer facing the harsh realities of his chosen profession. What must her father have been like at that age?

"Your mother was so worried about me," Gabe continued, his voice thick with emotion. "But eventually, you learn to cope. You find a way to compartmentalize, to put up a barrier between your work and your personal life."

"Is that what you did?" Sheila asked, genuinely curious.

"Most of the time," he admitted. "But some cases still haunt me. The ones that never got solved, or where justice wasn't served…those are the ones that keep me up at night."

Sheila felt a pang of sympathy for her father. She suspected he was also thinking about the death of her mother, Henrietta, which had never been solved.

"Thanks for sharing that, Dad," she said softly.

"Absolutely. Now, why don't you tell me about the case you're dealing with now? Talking always helped me process things."

She took a deep breath and let it out slowly, considering where to start. She decided to keep it simple.

"Three female college students have been found dead in three different colleges," she said, trying to remain neutral as she recounted the facts of the case. "Each of them was stabbed to death and shut in their lockers. I think maybe they were bullying someone, and that person got revenge by killing them."

Gabe's thoughtful silence on the other end of the call seemed to stretch on for an eternity. Then finally he spoke, his voice low and measured. "That certainly sounds like a possibility. But you need to be careful not to jump to conclusions. Throughout my years in law enforcement, I've seen many cases where investigators made assumptions without even realizing it, and those assumptions led them down the wrong path."

Sheila frowned, considering her father's words. "But what else could connect these victims? There must be something we're missing."

"Sometimes the connections aren't obvious at first glance," Gabe said. "Look for patterns in their behavior, their social circles, any recent changes in their lives. And remember, sometimes the most crucial clue is hiding in plain sight."

Sheila nodded slowly, though her father couldn't see it. His advice resonated with her, reminding her that there was still much to learn in this new chapter of her life. As she mulled over her father's words, she couldn't help but think about how closely she'd followed in his footsteps— both in kickboxing and now in law enforcement. And yet, despite their shared interests and experiences, she still felt like the outsider in their family, the daughter who could never quite measure up to her father's expectations.

Or had that changed, now that Natalie was the injured one, the limited one? She took no joy in the thought.

"Thanks, Dad," she said softly, her voice tinged with gratitude. "I'll keep all that in mind while we continue investigating."

"Good, Sheila. Just remember: assumptions can be dangerous. Keep an open mind and stay focused on the facts. And don't hesitate to reach out if you need advice or a sounding board."

"Will do," Sheila said, feeling a renewed sense of purpose. She knew that it would take time, effort, and a keen eye for detail to crack this case, but with her father's guidance and support, she felt confident that she could rise to the challenge.

"Take care of Natalie too, okay? She needs your support now more than ever."

"Of course, I will," she promised before hanging up the phone.

As she started walking again, she replayed the conversation she'd just had with Her father. His words about assumptions echoed in her head, and she suddenly realized she'd made one from the very beginning.

With renewed energy, Sheila hurried back to the cafeteria. As she entered, she found Natalie and Finn huddled together, talking in low voices.

"Guys!" Sheila said, excitement edging her voice. Their heads snapped up, curiosity flaring in their eyes. "I think we've been making a huge assumption this entire time!"

Natalie frowned, confused. "What do you mean?"

"All this time," she said, "we've been assuming the killer is a college girl who got bullied by the victims."

"You don't think she got bullied?" Natalie asked.

Sheila shook her head impatiently. It's not that. I don't think our killer is a *girl*."

CHAPTER SEVENTEEN

Sheila shifted her weight from one foot to the other as she stood in the office of Clearwater University's president, Moses Okafor, watching as he pulled up a video on his computer. Her impatience bubbled beneath the surface, making it hard for her to focus on anything other than the information they were about to uncover.

What's this about, anyway? she wondered. *We just asked him for any information he had on male students here at Clearwater who had filed complaints about bullying. So what's he doing on social media?*

As she waited, she glanced around the room, taking in the rich mahogany bookshelves that lined the walls and the diplomas and accolades displayed prominently. The office exuded a sense of sophistication and authority that matched the man seated behind the desk.

Moses was a large African-American man with a pointed beard that framed his strong jawline. His dark eyes were focused intently on the computer screen in front of him, his brow furrowed in concentration. As he typed, the muscles in his broad shoulders flexed under the tailored suit he wore, giving away the athletic build hidden underneath.

Sheila's sister, Natalie, sat in her wheelchair beside her, her face expressionless as she patiently waited for Moses to find what he was looking for. Finn leaned against a nearby bookshelf, his arms crossed over his chest. He hid his keen interest behind a casual demeanor, but Sheila knew better. All three of them were eager to discover any new leads in the murder case they were working on.

"Almost got it," Moses said, breaking the silence that had settled over the room. Sheila caught herself holding her breath and let out a quiet exhale, her fingers tapping rhythmically against her thigh.

"Take your time," Natalie said. "To be honest, I was surprised to find you were still here. It's quite late."

Moses looked up from the screen, offering her a weary smile. His eyes were heavy with fatigue, yet they held a spark of determination. He was a large man, his stature imposing, but there was a gentleness in his demeanor that made him approachable.

"Given the circumstances, it's hard for me to go home and rest comfortably," he said, adjusting his pointed beard with a sigh. "I've been on the phone nonstop, talking to parents, organizing meetings with faculty... We can't just carry on like nothing happened."

Natalie nodded solemnly, her expression one of understanding. Sheila marveled at her sister's ability to empathize, even when she herself was grappling with her own challenges—challenges Sheila knew she'd never fully comprehend.

Moses suddenly leaned back in his chair, his eyes still locked on the screen. "Found it," he said, his voice deep and commanding. He motioned for the trio to gather around the computer, and they eagerly complied.

The video that played before them showed a raucous party in full swing, the laughter and music almost tangible as they watched. Young people danced and chatted, their faces flushed with excitement and the unmistakable haze of intoxication. The cameraman weaved through the crowd, joking about making a documentary on getting high.

"There were forty or fifties kids in total," Moses said. "Students from Clearview, Coldwater Community, Elbridge College, and other local campuses. Lots of kids who went to high school together and then kept in touch."

"Everyone seems to be having a good time, but what does this have to do with the case?" Sheila asked, her eyes scanning the screen for any hint of a connection. With each passing second, her heart picked up its pace, fueled by a mix of adrenaline and curiosity.

"Keep watching," Moses said. "You'll understand soon enough."

The cameraman – a teenager, by the sound of him – continued his antics, moving through the crowded house with an easy swagger. As he reached a quieter section, he paused and turned the camera on himself, tilting his head to listen to the faint sounds of laughter and chatter from outside. A conspiratorial grin spread across his face.

"Let's see what kind of trouble they're getting into back here," he whispered, chuckling softly as he crept toward the backyard.

Sheila leaned in closer, her heart pounding in anticipation. The camera rounded the corner of the house, and the scene that unfolded before them sent a jolt down her spine.

Two college girls were tying a scrawny, mousy-faced young man to a tree, their fingers deftly working the knots as he protested weakly. "Please, just let me go," he whined, a note of desperation in his voice.

Natalie's gaze sharpened, her jaw clenched. "That's Ami Nasir and Jane Johnson," she said. "Two of the victims."

"Look at him," Finn muttered, his eyes narrowing as he studied the young man. "He's got to be humiliated."

"Hey, what's going on here?" the cameraman called out, amusement evident in his voice.

Jane looked up, a teasing smile playing on her lips. "Well, you see, we felt bad for Kyle here. Thought we'd show him a good time, and he agreed to come along for the ride." She gestured toward the blindfold lying nearby. "We led him out here, blindfolded, and before he knew what was happening, we had him tied up like this."

"Are you having fun, Jane?" Ami asked, a wicked grin on her face.

"Absolutely," Jane replied, her eyes twinkling mischievously. "Just like we promised Kyle."

Sheila's gaze shifted from the unsettling video to Moses, her voice urgent. "Who is Kyle? What do we know about him?"

Moses stroked his pointed beard thoughtfully before answering. "Kyle's full name is Kyle Benedict. He's a senior at Clearview University, majoring in computer science. Brilliant kid, but he's got some social...limitations. He's been bullied since he started here, poor guy."

As the room absorbed the information, Sheila could practically hear her sister's calculated gears turning next to her. She pictured Kyle, bound and humiliated, and her heart clenched with sympathy. He must have been mortified.

"Anyway," Moses continued, "this incident at the party happened just a few days ago. I've been debating whether or not to intervene, whether to talk to those involved or let them handle it on their own. It's a tough call."

Finn's fingers drummed on the desk, his brow furrowed as he analyzed the situation. "Maybe Kyle decided to sort it out himself," he said slowly, his tone dark. "By killing Ami and Jane."

CHAPTER EIGHTEEN

Sheila's stomach did an uneasy somersault as she, Natalie, and Finn pulled up in front of the Benedict home, the van's headlights illuminating the quiet suburban scene. She couldn't shake the memory of the last time she and Natalie were in a situation like this and the injury that had crippled her sister.

She had promised herself, and her father, that she would look after Natalie. But how could she do that? She couldn't control what would happen. What if Kyle was holed up in that house, armed to the teeth? No matter how proficient Natalie might be in her wheelchair, she would be at a huge disadvantage.

Then you'll just have to make sure she's not in harm's way, Sheila told herself as a wave of fierce determination washed over her. No matter what, she would not let Natalie get hurt again because of her.

Sheila turned off the engine, and the three of them sat in the darkness for a moment, taking in the late-night stillness of the neighborhood. The street was lined with neat lawns and well-kept houses, each one appearing as if it held secrets behind its closed doors. The Benedicts' house was no exception, its dark windows and silent facade giving nothing away. There was an attached garage, but from their vantage point, it was impossible to tell if any vehicles were inside.

The quiet surrounding them was almost unnerving, punctuated only by the distant barking of a dog or the rustling of leaves in the gentle breeze. It seemed surreal that they were about to confront a potential murderer in such a peaceful setting.

Natalie pressed a button on the van's control panel, and the door slid open with a soft hum. The mechanical lift whirred to life, lowering her wheelchair gently onto the pavement. Sheila stepped out of the van, her eyes darting between Natalie and the quiet house before them. The weight of her concern was heavy in her chest, and she couldn't help but voice it.

"Are you sure you want to come with us?" she asked, her brows furrowed with worry. "Maybe you should stay in the van, just in case."

Natalie shook her head firmly, the glint of determination in her eyes unyielding. "I'm the sheriff, Sheila," she said. "I'm not going to hide while my deputies do the actual police work."

Sheila glanced at Finn, who was frowning as well, his own concern mirroring hers. She exhaled slowly, trying to let go of her anxiety. She couldn't force Natalie to stay behind any more than she could guarantee there would be no danger.

As the trio made their way toward the house, the stillness of the night seemed to press in around them. The only light came from the moon, casting eerie shadows across the manicured lawns that lined the street. Sheila felt as though they were intruding on some hidden world, where secrets were whispered between the rustling leaves and shadows danced beneath the watchful gaze of the moon.

Finn raised his hand and knocked on the door, the sound seeming to reverberate through the quiet neighborhood. They waited, but there was no response. He knocked again, louder this time, and Sheila noticed movement in one of the windows.

"Hey, I think I saw something," she whispered, moving closer to the window for a better look.

Just as she leaned in, a large, vicious-looking dog lunged at the glass, its snarls and barks muffled by the barrier between them. Sheila stumbled back, her heart pounding in her chest as adrenaline flooded her system.

"Damn it," she muttered, trying to catch her breath. "Didn't expect that."

A light flickered on the second floor, cutting through the darkness like a knife. The sound of footsteps creaking down the stairs reached Sheila's ears, and she tensed, her muscles coiled and ready to react. The front door slowly opened, revealing a middle-aged woman with disheveled hair and sleep-filled eyes. She wore a faded floral nightgown, and her expression displayed both confusion and irritation.

"Wha-what do you want?" she asked, rubbing her eyes in an attempt to wake herself up fully.

"Mrs. Benedict?" Finn asked.

"Yes, that's me," the woman replied, her gaze darting among the trio of officers.

"We're looking for your son, Kyle," Finn continued, watching as the woman's eyes narrowed defensively.

"Kyle?" She took a long look at Finn's uniform and crossed her arms. "What do you want with him?"

"We just need to ask him some questions. Is he home?"

The woman hesitated, studying Finn skeptically. "You show up here, late at night, and demand to see my son—"

"We're not trying to make any demands, ma'am. We just need to—"

"And you won't even explain what it's about?" Mrs. Benedict turned to Sheila as if hoping that she at least might be reasonable. "Is this how you operate? Why didn't you come by earlier?"

It was clear that it wasn't easy for Mrs. Benedict to talk about her son. She seemed protective of him, which fit with his history of bullying. Perhaps she thought the police were out to get him, too.

"Ma'am," Sheila said patiently, hoping to defuse the tension, "we're more than happy to explain why we're here. I'm not sure if you're aware, but there was a recent incident at a party during which Kyle was tied to a tree by some other college students."

At the mention of the incident, Mrs. Benedict's face contorted with anger, her features hardening as she clenched her fists at her sides. "Those girls had no right to treat my son like that!" she said, her voice quivering with indignation. "Just because he prefers computers to sports or chasing after girls doesn't mean he deserves to be humiliated!"

Sheila couldn't help but feel a pang of sympathy for the woman; it was clear how much she cared for her son. "It's not right what they did to Kyle," she said. "He shouldn't have been targeted like that."

"Exactly!" Mrs. Benedict said, her passion evident. "My boy is brilliant; he's going to change the world someday. And those girls, they're just...just..." She struggled to find the words, her anger momentarily rendering her speechless.

"They're monsters," she finally finished, her eyes glistening with unshed tears. "And they deserve to be punished."

Sheila hesitated for a moment, choosing her words carefully. "That's the thing, Mrs. Benedict. Both of those girls are dead. Murdered."

Mrs. Benedict's face drained of color, and she looked as though she might collapse. Her eyes widened with shock, and she stared at Sheila with a mixture of disbelief and horror. "You don't think..." she whispered, her voice trembling. "You don't think Kyle had anything to do with it, do you?"

"Ma'am, we just need to talk to him," Finn said.

Natalie, who had remained silent so far during the exchange, spoke up. "Is Kyle home right now, Mrs. Benedict?"

"Y-yes," she stammered, still reeling from the revelation. "He's in the basement. I can take you there."

"Thank you," Natalie said. Mrs. Benedict opened the door wider and stepped back, allowing the officers to enter.

As they crossed the threshold, it suddenly occurred to Sheila that there was no ramp for the wheelchair. They would have to lift her up. She turned around, surprised to see that Finn had already realized this.

"Ready?" he asked, his hand resting lightly on the armrest of Natalie's wheelchair.

"On three," Sheila said, positioning herself on the other side of the chair. "One...two...three!"

With a grunt of effort, Sheila and Finn lifted Natalie's wheelchair, carefully maneuvering it up the few steps leading into the house. As they set the chair down gently, Natalie gave them a grateful smile. "Thanks, guys," she murmured, her cheeks flushed with a mixture of embarrassment and appreciation.

"Of course, sheriff," Finn said, tipping his cap.

The moment they stepped inside the house, Sheila was struck by the stark contrast between the dark exterior and the warm, lived-in atmosphere of the Benedict home. The walls were adorned with family photos, each capturing a different memory in time. A faint scent of lavender air freshener mingled with the unmistakable aroma of home-cooked meals that still lingered from dinner.

Suddenly, a large dog – the same one Sheila had seen at the window – came barreling down the hallway toward them, snarling and baring its teeth. Sheila's heart raced as she instinctively positioned herself between the dog and Natalie. But before the dog could reach them, Mrs. Benedict grabbed a broom from a nearby closet and swung it at the animal with surprising force. The dog yelped and retreated into an open bathroom, where Mrs. Benedict promptly shut the door, trapping the beast inside.

"Sorry about that," she said, her voice trembling slightly as she leaned the broom against the wall. "That's Brutus, Kyle's dog. He's usually not so aggressive."

Sheila offered a tight-lipped smile, her pulse still pounding in her ears. She glanced over at Finn, noticing how his hand hovered near his holstered gun despite the apparent resolution of the situation.

"Is everything alright down there?" a groggy male voice called from upstairs.

"Go back to sleep, dear," Mrs. Benedict replied without looking up. "It's got nothing to do with you." She turned her attention to her guests. "Please, follow me."

Mrs. Benedict said led the three of them to the basement stairs, then paused, glancing uncomfortably at Natalie.

"It's okay," Natalie said, smiling thinly. "I'll wait up here." Despite the smile, Sheila could hear the disappointment in her sister's voice. It had to frustrate her to be left behind like this. There was nothing to be done, however. Besides, Natalie was more than capable of handling herself.

"Kyle?" Mrs. Benedict called as she descended the stairs. "The police are here to talk to you."

Silence greeted them, and Sheila felt a shiver run down her spine.

"Kyle?" Mrs. Benedict's voice wavered as she called again, her desperation growing with each unanswered plea.

Sheila exchanged a concerned glance with Finn as they descended. Was Kyle still here, or had he heard them coming and taken off? Could he be on his way right now to attack his next victim?

The basement was a stark contrast to the rest of the house. The walls were plastered with posters of obscure bands and shelves filled with a mix of sci-fi novels, comic books, and figurines. There was a large computer desk cluttered with gadgets, cables, and half-built electronics projects. A gaming chair sat in front of the multiple monitors, where the glow of the paused game cast an eerie light on the room.

Sheila's eyes were immediately drawn to a corner where a collection of violent video games and graphic novels stood out like a sore thumb. She couldn't shake the feeling that there was more to Kyle than his nerdy exterior suggested.

"Kyle?" Mrs. Benedict called again, sounding less certain of a response every time she said his name. After a few more moments of searching, it became clear Kyle wasn't around.

"I'm sorry," she said, looking puzzled. "I could have sworn he was down here."

"Do you mind if we look around, Mrs. Benedict?" Finn asked.

"Please, do what you need to do."

As Sheila and Finn searched the room, Sheila noticed a corkboard covered in newspaper articles, photos, and strings connecting them all together—a bizarre conspiracy web. Her heart rate increased as she realized the articles were about the two murdered girls. At the center of the web, a disturbingly detailed drawing of one of the victims stared back at her, fear etched into the sketched face.

"Mrs. Benedict, have you seen this?" Sheila asked.

The woman approached, confusion apparent on her face. "I...I didn't know he had this. He never let me come down here."

"Mrs. Benedict," Finn said, "do you have any idea where Kyle might be?"

"No, I don't," she stammered, looking around the room in disbelief. "He's pretty much always down here. Doesn't really have friends, and since that incident, it's like he's afraid to show himself in public."

Examining the computer desk, Sheila spotted a scrap of paper partially hidden under a keyboard. She unfolded it, revealing a hastily scrawled message: "I HAVE TO DO SOMETHING TERRIBLE. I KNOW YOU WON'T UNDERSTAND, BUT I HOPE MAYBE SOME DAY YOU WILL FORGIVE ME."

"Mrs. Benedict," Sheila said urgently, showing her the note. "Do you have any idea what this means?"

The woman stared at it, looking more troubled by the second. "I have no idea. None of this is like him at all."

"What kind of vehicle does your son drive?" Finn asked.

"It's a red 2009 Honda Civic," she said, her voice shaking.

"Thank you," Sheila said, already heading back upstairs with Finn right behind her. Their search for Kyle had become far more urgent, and they couldn't afford to waste any more time.

At the top of the stairs, Sheila paused, looking for Natalie.

"Come on," Finn said, crossing the room in long strides. "We need to check the garage, see if his car's still here."

"Where's Natalie?"

"Probably back in the van." He waved a hand impatiently. "She'll be fine."

Sheila was not entirely satisfied by this hypothesis. Finn's sense of urgency, however, was contagious, and she hurried after him, heading outside and following the wall of the house to the garage, the door of which was closed.

Finn paused, drawing his weapon and looking back at Sheila. Then he counted on his hand: One, two, three.

On three, he threw the door open and stepped inside, Sheila right behind him. A silver SUV took up most of the room, the air of which smelled of oil and sawdust. Tools lay scattered on a workbench, and an array of old paint cans lined the shelves.

There was no red Honda Civic, however.

"Damn it," Sheila muttered under her breath.

"Must've already been gone when we arrived," Natalie said.

Sheila turned to see her sister in the corner of the room, rolling toward them.

"I figured I'd make myself useful," Natalie said, "and see if his vehicle was here."

"We need to put out an APB," Finn said, pulling out his phone.

"Already did," Natalie answered.

"How?" Sheila asked, surprised. "How did you know what he drove?"

Natalie gestured to a framed photo hanging on the wall. In it, a younger, shy-looking Kyle proudly leaned against his shiny, red car. His eyes locked onto the camera, as if silently pleading for approval.

One step ahead of me, even in a wheelchair, Sheila thought. Still, she supposed she ought to be grateful that her sister wasn't useless.

Just then, the radio at Natalie's side crackled to life. "Attention all units," a voice boomed, "suspect vehicle spotted heading westbound on Highway 89 at a high rate of speed."

For a moment, the three of them all looked at one another, frozen.

"Go!" Natalie shouted. "I'll stay here with Kyle's parents, see if they have any idea where he might be going."

Sheila hesitated, reluctant to leave her sister behind. "Are you sure?"

"I'll be fine, Sheila!" Natalie insisted. "I might be in a wheelchair, but that doesn't mean I can't kick your ass if you don't get moving."

That was all the encouragement Sheila needed. She rushed out of the garage, followed closely by Finn, and sprinted to the van, desperately hoping they wouldn't be too late to prevent another tragedy.

CHAPTER NINETEEN

The van's headlights sliced through the inky night as Sheila gripped the steering wheel, her eyes scanning the dark highway for any sign of Kyle Benedict's vehicle.

"Take the next right," Finn said, holding up his phone as he studied the GPS.

As she eased the van around the bend, Sheila couldn't help but dwell on the chilling message they had received from Kyle. He claimed he was going to do "SOMETHING TERRIBLE"—but what? The thought gnawed at her insides like a relentless itch. Was he planning to kill another college girl who had tormented him?

Finn grabbed the radio and spoke into it, urgency lacing his words. "Officer Daniels, do you still have eyes on the vehicle?"

A crackle of static preceded the weary reply. "Negative, Deputy Mercer. I lost sight of him about ten minutes ago. I've been doubling back, but no luck."

Sheila's stomach churned with unease, her heart sinking as she pictured Kyle slipping through their grasp like smoke through fingers. She swallowed hard, forcing herself to focus on the task at hand.

"Wait!" she exclaimed suddenly, her pulse quickening. Through the dim glow of the headlights, she noticed fresh tracks scarring the gravel shoulder. It seemed as if something had veered off the road at breakneck speed. She slowed the van, following the trail with her eyes until they settled on a twisted mass of metal wrapped around a tree.

"Over there!" She pointed at the mangled vehicle. "That's got to be him!"

She and Finn exchanged a tense glance before scrambling out of the vehicle. The air was thick with the scent of damp leaves and freshly churned earth. A chorus of crickets and frogs filled the night, their voices melding into an eerie, dissonant song.

"Stay behind me," Finn said, his voice low and cautious as he drew his weapon. Sheila nodded, her eyes scanning the desolate stretch of highway that plunged into darkness beyond the reach of the van's headlights. Tall, shadowy trees loomed over them, their branches outstretched like skeletal fingers. To their right, the ground dropped away sharply, forming the edge of a ravine that seemed to devour the light.

The crashed vehicle before them was barely recognizable, its metal frame twisted and torn. Glass shards littered the ground, glinting like stars against the dark earth. It looked as though it had been crushed in the jaws of some massive beast, so complete was its destruction.

"Kyle!" Finn called out as they approached the wreckage. "Are you in there?"

Sheila peered through the windows of the vehicles, worried what she might find. To her surprise, however, the vehicle was empty. The only sign that Kyle had ever been in there was the pattering of blood on the deflated airbag that covered the steering wheel.

Nosebleed, she thought.

She glanced around, searching for any sign of where Kyle had gone. The surrounding woods, however, offered no answers, only more questions.

"Where is he?" she asked, puzzled.

Finn shook his head grimly, holstering his weapon. "I don't know," he replied, frustration evident in his tone. "But we need to find him before he does something irreversible."

Sheila nodded, her mind racing with possibilities. If Kyle was still out there, desperate and alone, there was no telling what he might do. The weight of their responsibility pressed down on her like a heavy stone, threatening to crush her resolve. But she couldn't – wouldn't – let that happen. They had to find him, and they had to do it now.

As Sheila pondered where Kyle might have gone, she felt an inexplicable pull toward the ravine, as if some unseen force were guiding her. She approached it cautiously, her heart pounding in her chest. Peering over the edge, she found herself staring into a void of darkness that seemed to stretch down into eternity, its steep and jagged walls lined with craggy rocks and twisted branches that threatened to snag and tear at anyone foolish enough to venture too close.

"Kyle got lucky," she said softly, turning back to look at the mangled vehicle and the highway beyond. "If that tree hadn't been there, he would've gone right over the edge."

Finn eyed the ravine warily. "You think he could've climbed out of the car after the crash? Maybe he wandered off in a daze and fell in?"

"It's possible," Sheila said, her mind racing as she tried to imagine what might have happened. "He wouldn't be the first one to make a mistake like that, especially if he was disoriented or under the influence. It's equally possible, though, that he went back to the highway and flagged down a ride."

"Let's take a closer look," Finn suggested, pulling a flashlight from his belt and shining it down into the abyss. The beam illuminated the treacherous terrain below, a chaotic jumble of broken rocks, tangled roots, and dense foliage that appeared to swallow any trace of light.

"Look." Sheila pointed, her gaze catching on something in the shadows. "There's a slope leading down. It's steep, but it looks like we could get to the bottom."

Finn frowned, looking uncertain. "You really think he's down there?"

"If someone picked him up, he's long gone by now. This at least gives us a shot at finding him."

Finn worked his jaw back and forth, thinking. At last, he sighed and nodded. "Alright," he said. "But be careful—there's no need getting ourselves killed just to find his body."

They began the descent down the steep slope. Loose rocks and dirt shifted beneath their feet, testing their balance and resolve. The air grew colder, dampening their skin as beads of sweat formed on their brows.

"Kyle!" Sheila called, her voice strained from the effort of keeping herself upright. "We're here to help you! If you can hear me, just—" Suddenly her foot gave way beneath a loose stone, and she found herself stumbling forward, ready to somersault into the pit.

Just then, however, Finn reached out and, with lightning-fast reflexes, grabbed her arm and steadied her. Their eyes met for a moment.

"Like I said," he repeated, "no need getting ourselves killed."

"Thanks," Sheila muttered, regaining her footing.

At last, they reached the bottom of the ravine, where an eerie stillness prevailed. A shallow stream crawled through the rocky terrain, its waters glinting like veins of silver in the moonlight. Trees loomed overhead, casting dark shadows that stretched across the ground like grasping hands.

"Nothing," Finn said, frustration evident in his voice. "I can't see any sign of him."

"Keep looking," Sheila insisted.

"Wait," Finn said, holding up a finger as his phone rang. He answered, nodding as Natalie's voice came through the speaker. "Yeah,

Nat, we're there now. No sign of him yet." He paused, listening. "I know, but we can't give up on him. We have to try."

As Finn spoke with Natalie, Sheila continued her search, tuning out their conversation. Her gaze darted between the shadows, seeking any hint of movement or life. And then, just as she was about to give up hope, her eyes caught a glimpse of something pale and motionless.

"Hey!" she shouted, her heart pounding in her chest. "I think I found something!"

"Stay there," Finn said, ending the call with Natalie. "I'm coming."

Sheila's heart raced as she rushed toward the pale, lifeless hand protruding from the shadows.

"Kyle!" she called, her voice desperate and raw. She dropped to her knees beside him, her hands shaking as she reached out to examine his crumpled form.

"Over here, Finn!" she shouted, her eyes never leaving Kyle. "Call an ambulance!"

Kyle lay on the cold ground, his body twisted at an unnatural angle. His scrawny frame was barely visible under a layer of dirt and blood, and his face was a mask of pain and confusion. One of his legs was bent unnaturally, clearly broken, and a jagged wound marred his forehead, blood oozing sluggishly down the side of his face. Despite his injuries, he was still breathing, albeit shallowly.

"Hey," Sheila said. "You're going to be okay, alright? Just stay with me."

Kyle's glassy eyes fluttered open, and he looked at her with an expression of anguish. "I...I'm sorry," he said.

"Sorry for what?"

I never meant to hurt anyone," he groaned, his words slurred and barely audible. "It was all just a fantasy—it wasn't really supposed to happen."

CHAPTER TWENTY

Sheila stared at the dull, flickering fluorescent lights of the hospital waiting room, her gaze unfocused and her thoughts racing. The sterile scent of disinfectant and the low murmur of hushed conversations filled the air around her. Her right leg jittered restlessly, the rhythmic tapping of her foot betraying her impatience.

As a former Olympic kickboxer, she was no stranger to hospitals, but this visit was different. This time, the life of their prime suspect hung in the balance.

The door to the waiting room creaked open, and Natalie wheeled herself in. Her dark hair was pulled into a tight ponytail, and her eyes were sharp with determination as they scanned the room. Despite her injury, she exuded an aura of authority—a sheriff who refused to be held back by her physical limitations.

"Is he still alive?" she asked, her voice tense.

"Kyle's stable for now," Sheila said, her gaze meeting Natalie's. "But it's unclear when he'll wake up. His leg was broken from the fall, and he sustained other injuries as well. The doctors are concerned he might slip into a coma."

Sheila's chest tightened at the thought. If Kyle fell into a coma, they might never get the answers they desperately needed. Their investigation hinged on what he knew, and even though it seemed there was a good chance Kyle was the one responsible for the murders, they wouldn't know until they had a chance to speak with him.

"Damn," Natalie muttered under her breath, her hands gripping the wheels of her chair tightly. "We can't afford to lose him."

Sheila nodded, her heart heavy with frustration. She glanced over at Finn, who stood silently near the window, his tall form casting a long shadow across the linoleum floor. The deputy's eyes were distant, unreadable as his fingers brushed at his sternum, stroking the compass necklace hidden beneath the fabric.

What's he thinking? Sheila wondered, wishing she could ask him. *And what's the deal with that necklace?* Had she been alone with him, she might very well have asked both questions, but she didn't want to put him on the spot in front of Natalie. Knowing how reserved and private a person he seemed to be, she had a feeling he would only change the topic, perhaps telling a joke or bringing up something about the case.

She would just have to find an opportunity when they were alone.

It was past midnight, and the once bustling hospital had quieted significantly. The only sounds that punctured the silence were the beeping of distant machines, the occasional footsteps of a nurse or doctor, and the ticking of an old clock above the reception desk.

As they waited, Sheila's gaze drifted to her sister, noticing the subtle tension in Natalie's shoulders as she maneuvered her wheelchair closer. The sterile smell of antiseptic and the faint hum of fluorescent lights brought back memories that sent a shiver down Sheila's spine.

She found herself thinking back to when Natalie had been shot a month ago, and the panicked rush to get her to the hospital. She could still feel the cold metal of the ambulance railing beneath her fingers as she clung to it, holding Natalie's hand tightly. The blaring siren had been deafening, but not nearly as loud as the panicked voice screaming that she might lose her sister forever.

They'd spent hours in another waiting room, just like this one, their dad and brother pacing like caged animals while Natalie was in surgery. After what felt like an eternity, they took turns sitting beside her bed, watching for any sign of movement or consciousness. It was one of the scariest experiences of Sheila's life, and the stark white walls and clinical atmosphere of this hospital brought it all rushing back.

Lost in her thoughts, Sheila didn't immediately register the sound of a door opening. She looked up to see a doctor stepping into the waiting area, his face grave and tired. He was a tall man, middle-aged, with salt-and-pepper hair and a pair of wire-rimmed glasses perched on his prominent nose.

"Doctor," Finn said, drawing the man's attention. "What news do you have?"

The doctor approached them, adjusting his glasses as he spoke. "Mr. Benedict's condition is stable, but he's sustained significant injuries from the car crash and his fall into the ravine. His leg is broken in two places, and he has multiple contusions and lacerations."

"Is he awake?" Sheila asked.

"Remarkably, yes," the doctor replied, a hint of amazement in his tone. "All things considered, it's a miracle he's alive, let alone conscious. He's groggy from the pain medication, but he should be able to talk."

Sheila exchanged a glance with Finn and Natalie. This was their chance to get some answers. They needed to know if Kyle was truly responsible for the murders that had shaken their small town. As she rose from her seat, determination coursed through her veins. She would not let fear or uncertainty hold her back—not when the truth was finally within reach.

They followed the doctor through the sterile hospital corridors. As they turned a corner, the faint sound of distant beeping from medical equipment reached Sheila's ears, a reminder of the frailty of life that surrounded them. She glanced at her sister, noting the determined set of Natalie's jaw as she propelled her wheelchair forward. If not for that iron determination, Natalie might still be in a hospital just like this one, instead of doing what she loved and serving her community.

That's Natalie, Sheila thought. *She never stops pushing herself.*

At last, they arrived at Kyle's room. The doctor pushed the door open, revealing a small room filled with the steady hum of machines monitoring the young man's vital signs. Kyle lay in bed, his scrawny frame dwarfed by the surrounding medical apparatus. His once messy brown hair was now matted with sweat, and dark circles marred the skin beneath his bloodshot eyes. A look of shame and exhaustion was etched into his pale face, making him appear even more vulnerable than before.

"Thank you, doctor," Natalie said as the physician nodded and took his leave, closing the door behind him.

"Hello, Mr. Benedict," Natalie said, striking a professional tone. "I'm Sheriff Natalie Stone. This is my sister, Sheila, and our colleague, Deputy Mercer. We're here to talk to you about what happened."

A flicker of confusion crossed Kyle's features. "Why are there three of you?" he asked, his voice weak and raspy. "Isn't that a bit much?"

"Never mind that," Natalie said, evading the question. "Are you up for talking?"

"Can't sleep anyway," Kyle muttered, wincing as he shifted his position. "Painkillers aren't doing much, so we might as well get this over with."

"Where were you driving to when you crashed?" Natalie asked.

Kyle looked away, as if avoiding their gaze would shield him from whatever judgment they might pass. "I just...I needed some fresh air," he said evasively. "Clear my head, y'know? I was listening to music, and it was loud, so I didn't realize how fast I was going." He paused, swallowing hard. "I reached to turn up the volume, and...I drove off the road. I got out of the car, and that's when I fell into the ravine."

Sheila scrutinized Kyle's face as he finished his story, her instincts flaring with doubt. She knew there was more to the situation than what he had revealed, and she couldn't shake the feeling that he was hiding something important.

"Kyle," she said slowly, carefully choosing her words, "we found a note you left for your parents. It said you were sorry for having to do 'SOMETHING TERRIBLE.' What did you mean by that?"

The question seemed to catch him off guard, and his eyes darted nervously around the room, searching for an escape. After a moment, he laughed—a brittle, hollow sound that sent a chill down Sheila's spine. "It was just a joke," he stammered, beads of sweat forming on his brow.

Sheila exchanged glances with Natalie and Finn, seeing in their expressions that they, too, were unconvinced. But before she could press further, Kyle's face paled, and he clutched at his chest. "I'm not feeling well," he gasped, his breath shallow and uneven. "Can you...can you please leave me alone?"

Finn stepped closer to the bed, his expression hardening into a steely resolve. He leaned down, his voice low and dangerous. "Don't play games with us, kid. We know about the bullying incident, how you were tied to that tree. We've seen the video."

At Finn's words, Kyle's eyes narrowed, his anger boiling to the surface as he recalled that humiliating night. "Those girls...they tricked me," he said, bitterness lacing his words. "Lured me in with promises of a good time, only to tie me up like some animal for everyone at the party to laugh at. It was...it was unbearable." He clenched his fists, his knuckles turning white from the intensity of his grip.

Sheila could see the pain in Kyle's expression, but she couldn't let her sympathy cloud her judgment. She needed to know the truth, and so did Finn and Natalie. Finn pressed further, his voice firm yet cautious. "So, what did you do to get back at them?"

For a moment, it seemed as if Kyle might confess to the murders. His eyes darted around the room, avoiding their gazes. But then, with a shaky breath, he revealed his retaliation. "I got my revenge online. I wrote posts about them on a college forum, trying to scare them, make them feel as vulnerable as they made me feel when I was tied to that tree."

"Can you show us proof of these posts?" Natalie asked.

Kyle hesitated, growing visibly wary. His gaze flickered between the three of them, uncertainty clouding his features. "What happens to me if I do?" he finally asked.

Finn's eyes narrowed, his voice taking on a hardened edge. "Kyle, you're on the hook for murder. Your best defense right now is to be completely honest with us."

Surprise flashed across Kyle's face, and he shook his head vigorously. "I didn't kill anyone," he insisted, but there was an underlying tremor in his voice that betrayed his fear.

Sheila locked her gaze onto him, unwilling to let him off the hook so easily. "Then where were you driving to in such a hurry?" she asked.

Kyle opened his mouth to speak, but hesitated as he caught the steely determination in Sheila's eyes. "Like I said before, I needed some fresh air."

"Stop lying, Kyle," she said, her voice like ice. "Tell us the truth."

For a moment, silence hung heavy in the room. Kyle's eyes darted around, as if searching for someone to intervene, to free him from this relentless interrogation. Then, looking utterly defeated, he lowered his gaze to the stark white sheets covering his bruised body.

"I couldn't take it anymore," he admitted, his voice cracking with shame. "The humiliation, the constant torment...I was going to kill myself." He swallowed hard, tears threatening to spill over. "I meant to drive right into the ravine, but I hit a tree instead. That's what the 'TERRIBLE SOMETHING' in the note to my parents was about."

A heavy silence settled over the room, broken only by the faint, rhythmic beeping of the heart monitor beside Kyle's bed. Sheila exchanged a somber look with Finn and Natalie, the weight of Kyle's confession pressing down on them all.

Kyle laughed bitterly. "I couldn't even kill myself properly. How pathetic is that?"

"For what it's worth," Sheila said, "I don't think you killed anyone. But the only way we can be sure of that is if you cooperate with us. You don't want your friends and family thinking you're a murderer, do you?"

Kyle stared at her, chewing his lip. He seemed to be caught between a rock and a hard place.

Natalie cleared her throat. "We still need proof of those posts you wrote, Kyle. Can you show us?"

Kyle stared at Sheila a few seconds longer before coming to a decision. Taking a shaky breath, he nodded. "They're on my blog. You shouldn't have any trouble finding them." He gave Natalie the web address.

As Natalie pulled up the page on her phone, Sheila and Finn leaned in, their eyes scanning the screen.

There they were: the posts Kyle had written, full of cruel rumors about Jane Johnson and Ami Nasir. They contained threats, and even fake pictures of the girls making out with different students—a disturbing attempt at humiliating them like they had humiliated him.

As the three of them stood there, taking in the evidence of Kyle's twisted revenge, a chilling realization settled over Sheila. The depths of human cruelty seemed endless.

Sheila studied Kyle's face, searching for any hint of deception in his desperate eyes. The room felt colder now, the steady beeping of the heart monitor a chilling reminder of the fragile line between life and death.

"Kyle," she began, "we need to know where you were earlier this evening. Can anyone vouch for your whereabouts?"

"Y-yes," he stammered, his hands twisting the thin hospital sheets. "I was in my room, in my parents' basement, all day until I went for that drive."

"Can your parents confirm that?" Sheila asked, watching him closely.

He nodded, desperation seeping into his voice. "Yes, they were home all day. They can vouch for me."

Finn stepped forward, his brow furrowed in suspicion. "But your parents didn't even notice when you drove off, did they? There's no telling when you might have left."

A flicker of panic crossed Kyle's face, and he licked his dry lips. "No, but I swear I was there! Please, you have to believe me."

The room seemed to close in around them, the shadows cast by the dim hospital light growing darker with each passing second. Sheila could feel the uncertainty gnawing at her insides, leaving her torn between wanting to believe Kyle's story and the nagging feeling that something wasn't quite right.

She glanced at Finn and Natalie, their expressions mirroring her own inner turmoil. As the silence stretched on, Sheila found herself grappling with questions she couldn't answer, pulled in different directions by the need for justice and the fear of condemning an innocent man.

"Please," Kyle whispered again, his voice cracking under the weight of his plea. "I didn't kill anyone. I just wanted to die."

But was he telling the truth? Or was this just another lie? Sheila didn't know.

She did know one thing for certain, however. They needed to get to the bottom of this soon, because if the real killer was still out there, there was no telling when he might strike again.

CHAPTER TWENTY ONE

Sheila leaned against the cold hospital wall outside Kyle's room, her eyelids heavy and her body aching for rest. She rubbed her temples, trying to ease the dull throbbing pain that had taken residence in her head. The fluorescent lights above cast an unforgiving glare on her face, highlighting the exhaustion etched into her features.

"Are we sure we're not just chasing our tails here?" she asked Natalie and Finn, who flanked her in the hallway. "I mean, what if Kyle isn't our guy?"

Finn crossed his arms, his brow furrowed in thought. "His alibi certainly doesn't hold water. He could've slipped out of his house without his parents noticing, not to mention the fact that he's been lying to us from the start."

As Natalie maneuvered her wheelchair closer, Sheila couldn't help but admire her sister's determination. Despite her own physical challenges, Natalie always seemed to carry on without complaint. "The question is how much he's lied, and whether or not he's still lying," Natalie said. "We need to go back to his room and investigate more carefully for any clues that might suggest he's the killer."

Sheila shifted her weight, feeling the familiar sting of sibling rivalry bite at her. She wanted to prove herself, to be as useful and vital to this investigation as her decorated sister. But her body was rebelling against her, every muscle screaming for the sweet release of sleep.

"Alright," she said, stifling a yawn. "Let's get to the bottom of this, then."

Natalie's keen gaze settled on Sheila, her eyes narrowing slightly. "Sheila," she said gently, her voice surprisingly tender, "why don't you head home and get some rest? We'll be fine here."

Sheila shook her head. She didn't like quitting while others kept working. "I can handle it, Nat," she said.

Natalie's wheelchair squeaked softly as she adjusted her position. "Look, you're not an official police officer. Besides, we can let you know if there are any developments."

As much as Sheila hated the idea of leaving while they did all the work, she couldn't deny that her body was practically screaming for sleep. Her eyelids felt like they were being weighed down by lead, and her legs trembled with fatigue. Grudgingly, she admitted to herself that she would be much sharper if she got a little rest.

"Fine," she relented, exhaling a heavy sigh. She fished the keys to the van out of her pocket and handed them to Finn, who in turn passed her the keys to his vehicle.

"Be careful with my ride," Finn said. "She's like a daughter to me." He winked to show he wasn't entirely serious.

"Take care of yourself, Sheila," Natalie said. "We need you at your best."

Sheila nodded, swallowing the lump that had formed in her throat. As she watched Natalie and Finn move off, she couldn't help but feel a twinge of envy toward their unwavering partnership. She wished she could be more like them—strong, determined, and always ready to face whatever challenges came their way.

Her phone buzzed in her pocket, and she pulled it out to see an automated message from her wireless company updating her on a policy change. She ignored the message, but before closing her phone, she noticed a different message, one her father had sent earlier: *Hey, Sheila, if you're in the area, feel free to stop by. I'd love to see you.*

That's odd, Sheila thought. *When is he ever so...casual? Is there something going on that I don't know about?*

Whatever the case, it would be good to have somewhere to crash since her own house was still very much a work in progress.

She started walking again, following the hallway back to the waiting room and then taking the exit. The chilled night air bit at her skin as she stepped out of the hospital, but it did little to wake her. She trudged toward Finn's vehicle, each step feeling heavier than the last.

As she settled into the driver's seat, she vowed to herself that she wouldn't let her exhaustion get the better of her. She would rest up, clear her mind, and return to the investigation with renewed vigor—for the sake of the victims and for her own sense of purpose.

"Sleep," she whispered to herself, gripping the steering wheel tightly, "just a few hours, and then back to the case."

As she pulled the door of Finn's vehicle shut, however, she found herself thinking back to what Kyle had said in the hospital room. Her fingers danced across the steering wheel, the textured leather a stark contrast to the smooth metal of the keys in her other hand.

"Kyle," she muttered under her breath, feeling a knot tighten in her chest as she considered his claims. Was he telling the truth when he claimed he'd only harassed the victims online, rather than killing them?

She started the car and drove off, the engine's low hum accompanying her thoughts. As she navigated the dark streets, she couldn't shake the image of Kyle's frightened face when they interrogated him. What if there was more to his story? He'd been bullied, yes, which gave him motive, but he didn't seem like the kind of person who would actually confront his enemies to their faces. He seemed more like—

Well, like the type of person who would anonymously attack them online instead of attacking them in person.

Troubled by these thoughts, Sheila pulled over to the side of the road and grabbed her phone, her curiosity urging her to dig deeper. She navigated to Kyle's blog, the screen illuminating her face with an eerie glow. Her heart raced as she scrolled through the posts, each one a cruel reminder of the pain the victims had endured.

Ami deserved what happened to her, part of one post read. *She thought she was untouchable, but now everyone knows the truth.* Another post targeted a different victim: *Jane played with people's emotions like it was a game. Well, now it's game over for her.*

The venomous words seemed to seep from the screen, leaving a bitter taste in Sheila's mouth. Each post was a twisted mix of rumors and threats, all aimed at tearing down the victims and justifying their fates.

"Is this really just harassment, or is there something more?" she whispered. Her mind raced, trying to piece together the puzzle that lay before her.

Her gaze was drawn to the comments section beneath Kyle's posts. Some of these comments were even more vicious than the original posts, filled with hate and an insatiable thirst for retribution. *Jane got what she deserved,* one comment read. I *hope they all suffer like they made others suffer.*

Sheila's heart pounded in her chest, each beat echoing in her ears as the weight of the words on the screen settled into her soul. The cruel remarks seemed to multiply before her eyes, a cacophony of voices reveling in the pain and torment of the victims.

Can't wait for the next one to bite the dust, another commenter wrote, followed by a string of laughing emojis. *This town needs a good cleansing.*

There was something far more violent, far darker, about these comments than anything in the posts Kyle had written. These comments pulled no punches, made no efforts to tone down the vitriol. They were full of pure, unadulterated hate.

It was then that Sheila noticed something else, as well. Nearly all of the most hateful comments had been posted by the same user: DarkReaper88. The username sent a shiver down Sheila's spine.

Could this person be the real killer?

CHAPTER TWENTY TWO

The engine of Finn's car roared as Sheila pressed the accelerator, weaving through the dark, desolate streets. She could feel the leather steering wheel beneath her fingertips, gripping it tightly as she balanced her phone between her shoulder and ear.

The night sky was a blanket of blackness, pierced only by the headlights of the car and the occasional streetlight. Buildings and trees blurred together as she sped back toward Kyle Benedict's house.

"Come on, Natalie, pick up," Sheila muttered under her breath, her impatience growing with every unanswered ring. Her heart pounded in her chest, the rhythmic thumping echoing the urgency of her thoughts.

As the scenery raced by, illuminated by the car's headlights before being swallowed by darkness, Sheila's frustration continued to mount. She now believed that her sister and Finn were focusing their efforts on the wrong suspect, but how could she tell them if they wouldn't answer their phones?

Her grip on the steering wheel tightened, knuckles turning white. The car surged forward, its tires screeching against the pavement as she took a sharp turn. This wasn't just about proving a man's guilt anymore; lives were at stake, and every second wasted felt like an eternity.

"Damn it, Nat," she hissed, her breath fogging up the window for a moment before dissipating. "Where are you?"

The sound of the call connecting was abruptly followed by the beep of Natalie's voicemail. Sheila clenched her jaw, the muscles in her face tensing.

"Nat, it's me," she began, trying to keep her voice steady despite her mounting frustration. "I don't think Kyle is our guy. I have new information, but I need your help. Call me back as soon as you can."

Sheila exhaled sharply and ended the call. Gritting her teeth, she dialed Finn's number next. The rings were met with silence, and she knew his phone must be off—likely silenced during their interview with Kyle's parents. Her frustration bubbled over as she tossed the phone onto the passenger seat.

She groaned, gripping the steering wheel tighter. "What am I supposed to do now?"

The night outside was unforgiving, shadows cast by streetlights fleeing past as Sheila sped down the road. She could feel the urgency gnawing at her, and she knew that every second wasted brought the real killer one step closer to escaping. Going back to Kyle's house seemed like her only option, but the thought of wasting more time drove her mad.

As her mind raced, an idea struck her like a bolt of lightning. The blog—that online cesspool where she'd found all those hate-filled comments about the victims. Maybe there was a way to communicate directly with the person behind those comments to get him to reveal something about himself. It was risky, dangerous even, but it was the best shot she had.

"Okay," she muttered to herself, pulling over to the side of the road beneath the dim glow of a streetlight. "Let's give this a try."

Her hands trembled slightly as she picked up her phone again, fingers tapping rapidly on the screen to bring up the website. Sheila took a deep breath before diving into the process of creating an account on the blog. As she filled out the required fields, her heart pounded in her chest, a mix of fear and anticipation stirring within her.

By force of habit, she used her actual information: her email address, date of birth, name, and so on. Then, realizing it would be foolish to give away her identity, she decided to use a fake name instead: Sandra Peterson.

With her new account ready to go, Sheila navigated to the profile of the person she suspected to be the killer. The dim glow from her phone screen illuminated her face, casting eerie shadows across her determined expression. Her fingers trembled slightly as she scrolled through the hateful, threatening messages that had been left about each of the victims.

"Last online: 15 minutes ago," the profile stated. A glimmer of hope sparked within her—perhaps he was still awake, still reachable. But what could she say to grab his attention without sounding too eager or suspicious?

Sheila decided on a plan: she would pose as a fellow student who had connected the dots and knew he was the killer. More importantly, she would pretend to admire him for taking a stand against bullying, claiming to be a victim of it herself. That way, she could appeal to his twisted sense of justice and possibly unravel more information about him.

Taking a deep breath, she tapped out a message with calculated precision. *Hey there, I saw your posts about those stupid bullies. My name's Sandra, and I'm a first-year at Clearview. I've been bullied in the past, and I can't help but feel a sense of...relief knowing that someone is finally standing up for us.*

Sheila hesitated for a moment, then continued: *I've always been curious about the final moments of life—when the soul leaves the body and all that remains is an empty shell. It must be exhilarating to witness such a transformation up close. Maybe even empowering...*

As she immersed herself deeper into the role, Sheila felt a strange thrill in crafting this persona. She drew upon her own experiences of being sidelined and underestimated in life, weaving them into the fabric of her deception.

Anyway, she typed, continuing the message, *I've been following the news closely, and I have a feeling you might be the one responsible for all of this. If that's the case, I just want to say thank you. Thank you for taking a stand against those who have made our lives miserable.*

Her finger hovered over the 'send' button, heart pounding in her chest. This was it—the point of no return. With a surge of determination, Sheila pressed down, sending her message into the digital void.

"Come on, Sandra," she murmured to herself. "Let's see if you can catch a killer."

She sat back in the driver's seat. The night air was still and heavy, crickets chirping in the distance. She glanced at her surroundings, taking in the foliage that lined the side of the road. The shadows of tall trees swayed gently under the moonlight, casting eerie shapes onto the pavement. The occasional car rushed past her, headlights briefly illuminating the interior of Finn's car.

Her fingers drummed nervously on the steering wheel, a thousand thoughts racing through her mind. Had she just made a terrible mistake? What if her message had spooked him, sending him into hiding before they could catch him?

A pang of guilt twisted in Sheila's stomach, gnawing at her confidence. With each passing minute, her doubt grew stronger. In her desperation to solve the case, she wondered if she had inadvertently pushed the killer further out of reach.

As the minutes ticked by, Sheila began to lose hope. But then, her phone buzzed, jolting her from her anxious thoughts. A notification flashed across the screen: "New message."

Hello Sandra, the reply began. *I must say, your posts intrigued me. It's refreshing to find someone who understands the importance of justice. So many people are content to let wrongs go unpunished, but not you—or me, for that matter.*

Sheila's breath caught in her throat. This was it. She was communicating with the murderer. With trembling fingers, she typed her response, careful to maintain her alias.

I'm glad I found someone else who sees things the way I do, she wrote. *Your actions have left a significant impact on our community, and I can't help but admire your dedication to justice. I'd love to hear more about how you did it.*

She held her breath, waiting for his answer. Instead of the confirmation she sought, however, his reply was more cryptic: *Why don't we meet up? You can pick my brain all you want when we're face to face.*

Maybe this was as close to an admission of guilt as she was likely to get. Despite the lack of a clear confession, she felt in her bones that this was indeed the killer.

Her fingers hovered above her phone screen, uncertainty gnawing at her insides. Meeting this person alone was a dangerous gamble, but she couldn't shake her conviction that this was the only way to bring him to justice. She glanced around the shadowy roadside, the darkness punctuated by the occasional headlight from passing cars, and clenched her jaw.

"Think, Sheila," she muttered under her breath, feeling the weight of responsibility pressing down on her shoulders. She considered calling Natalie and Finn, but the memory of her sister's wheelchair-bound form flashed through her mind, guilt bubbling up inside her. No, she couldn't risk putting her in harm's way again.

She took a deep breath, trying to steady her nerves. Her thumb tapped out her response before she could second-guess herself any further.

Sounds like a plan. Where and when?

She hit send, then immediately regretted it. What if she had just signed her own death warrant? The seconds stretched into minutes as she waited for his reply, her pulse throbbing in her ears. She tried to focus on the cool night air against her skin, the distant hum of engines on the highway, but her thoughts were consumed by the potential consequences of her actions.

"Damn it, Sheila," she whispered, gripping the steering wheel tightly. "You better know what you're doing."

Finally, the response came: *Meet me by the old Coldwater steel mill. Parking lot.*

When? Sheila typed back, holding her breath.

As soon as you can get there, the stranger wrote back.

CHAPTER TWENTY THREE

Reagan sat hunched on a cold bench at the edge of the college campus, his fingers tapping an erratic beat against the metal armrest. The night air was thick with tension and anticipation as he stared at the glowing screen of his phone.

How had Sandra known about the murders? Her sudden contact had aroused both curiosity and confusion within him, leaving him feeling like a marionette on strings he couldn't see. He glanced around the deserted courtyard, shadows twisting into monstrous shapes under the dim streetlights.

"Who are you, really?" he muttered to himself, hoping for some kind of clarity in the darkness that enveloped him.

The sound of laughter shattered Reagan's thoughts. It drifted from a nearby girls' dorm, its windows spilling light onto the cobblestone path below. His eyes narrowed as he listened to their carefree voices, a sickening disgust curdling in his gut. Did they not realize what happened just this morning? Were they truly so wrapped up in their own shallow lives that murder meant nothing to them?

"Unbelievable," he said under his breath, his hands clenching into fists. The contrast between their obliviousness and the grisly reality of the crime scene made his blood boil. They laughed and chatted without a care while someone's life had been snuffed out like a candle in the wind.

In that moment, Reagan's anger consumed him. With each peal of laughter that reached his ears, the heat of his fury intensified. These girls were ignorant to the world around them, blind to the horrors lurking in the shadows. But soon, that would all change.

Navigating to the pictures on his phone, he examined the collection of photos he'd downloaded either from Deirdre's profile or from the profiles of her roommates, piecing them all together to get an idea of the inside of her dorm hall. He knew the size of the hall, knew how many rooms were there, knew which room was Deirdre's. The only thing he hadn't figured out yet was how to get in, but he was sure he could find a way.

He felt a twisted thrill at the thought of Deirdre becoming his next target. The craving for revenge swirled inside him like a venomous serpent, consuming every other thought in its path.

"Deirdre," he whispered to himself, feeling the name roll off his tongue like a dark promise. "I'll be seeing you soon."

It was only a matter of time before someone connected the dots, realizing what all the victims had in common, and then he would get the respect he deserved. Then, all those others who had tormented him would realize that none of them were safe.

Restless energy coursed through Reagan as he rose from the bench and approached the girls' dorm. His footsteps were deliberate and quiet, each step calculated to avoid making any noise that might alert someone to his presence. Shadows clung to him like a cloak, concealing him from any prying eyes.

Reagan's heart hammered in his chest as he stood by the dormitory, the cold night air pricking at his skin with a near-silent whisper. He had barely begun to form a plan for entering the building when the glaring lights of a police car sliced through the darkness, casting eerie streaks across the brick facade.

"Hey!" a man called, his voice cutting through the night like a blade. "What are you doing here?"

Reagan's pulse spiked, and his mouth went dry. He forced himself to swallow, pushing down the fear that threatened to choke him. "I, uh, was just taking a walk," he stammered, trying to sound nonchalant. "Couldn't sleep."

The officer leaned out the window of his patrol car, and Reagan realized with a shock that he recognized the man. It was Officer Daniels, whom he'd met that morning close to the locker where he'd left Kristen Lee's body. A thrill of fear went through Reagan.

Daniels narrowed his eyes, scrutinizing Reagan like a hawk eyeing its prey. "You know there's a curfew in place, right?"

"Of course," Reagan lied smoothly, struggling to keep his composure. "I didn't think it applied to me since I'm not a student." His mind raced, searching for anything that might convince Daniels of his innocence. "I'm visiting my cousin—she lives in the next building over. I just got lost, I guess."

"Really?" Daniels raised an eyebrow, clearly skeptical. "And what's your cousin's name?"

"Uh, Lisa," Reagan replied, the name slipping out before he could think about whether or not it sounded plausible. "Lisa Thompson."

Inside, Reagan berated himself for his lack of foresight. He should have prepared for this eventuality, but his single-minded focus on Deirdre had left him vulnerable. The weight of uncertainty bore down on him, twisting his stomach into knots as he tried to gauge whether or not Daniels believed his story.

"You do realize," Daniels asked, "male students aren't allowed in these dorms after dark, right?"

Reagan hesitated, unsure what to say. Just as the suspicion in Officer Daniels' eyes seemed to deepen, the crackle of his radio interrupted their tense conversation. "We need immediate assistance with a pursuit near Elm Street," the dispatcher's voice urgently requested.

"Copy that, I'm on my way," Daniels replied, his attention momentarily diverted from Reagan. He shot Reagan one last warning glance before putting the car in drive and speeding off. As the taillights faded into the distance, the siren wailing into the night, Reagan felt a wave of relief wash over him.

With Daniels gone, Reagan retreated into the shadows, his heart pounding in his ears. He had narrowly avoided being caught, but now he was more determined than ever to continue his plan. He found a secluded spot behind a large tree, its gnarled branches casting eerie silhouettes on the ground, and settled in to wait for Deirdre and her friends to fall asleep.

The air around him was heavy with anticipation, charged with an unsettling energy that prickled at his skin. The darkness seemed to close in around him, muffling the distant laughter of the college students and amplifying the rustle of leaves in the breeze. His breaths came shallow and quick, each exhale leaving a cloud of vapor in the cool night air.

As he crouched there, hidden in the gloom, Reagan couldn't help but let his thoughts wander to Deirdre, picturing her face contorted with fear when she realized what was happening. A sick thrill coursed through him at the thought, and he clenched his fists with anticipation.

"Get a grip," he muttered under his breath, trying to tamp down the growing excitement that threatened to consume him. He needed to stay focused, to remain patient until the perfect moment to strike presented itself.

As he waited, he found his mind wandering back to Sandra and the messages she'd left him. He pulled out his phone and stared at the glowing screen, reading what she'd said.

Your posts intrigued me. It's refreshing to find someone who understands the importance of justice. And *I can't help but admire your dedication to justice. I'd love to hear more about how you did it.*

Reagan basked in the praise, feeling a newfound connection to this mysterious woman who seemed to understand his motives. A grin stretched across his face as he scrolled through her texts, savoring each word.

But curiosity gnawed at him, a hunger that refused to be sated. Who was this Sandra? What was her story? And most importantly, could he trust her?

Determined to find out, Reagan put his tech-savvy skills to work. In the isolated silence of the night, his fingers danced across the screen, tracing the digital breadcrumbs back to their source.

It was a fairly simple procedure. Since she had registered as a user on his blog, he had access to her IP address and email address. By combining these two, he was able to discover her name: Sheila Stone. Then he looked up this name, and he soon found an article about an Olympic kickboxer of the same name.

A kickboxer who'd grown up in Coldwater, Utah. And who just happened to be the sister of Coldwater's sheriff.

Reagan's heart pounded in his chest, the satisfaction he had felt moments ago now replaced by a seething rage that threatened to boil over.

"Damn it!" he cursed under his breath, slamming his fist against the wall. The impact sent a jolt of pain up his arm, but it did little to quell the storm brewing within him.

He had been so careful, so methodical in his planning, and now he realized he was ensnared in a dangerous game. Every move he made, every victim he chose—it was all being watched, scrutinized by someone who held a position of power.

"Think, Reagan," he muttered to himself, his mind racing with possibilities. "What's her angle? Why is she toying with me like this?"

His thoughts were a whirlwind, a chaotic maelstrom that threatened to pull him under. He needed to learn more.

He tapped away at his phone again, and soon the screen displayed Sheila Stone's social media profile, her smiling face mocking him amidst images of her athletic achievements. As he scrolled through her posts with trembling fingers, he discovered that she, too, was one of those girls—the ones who reveled in their physical prowess, flaunting it without remorse or compassion for those they tormented. Those who had made his life a living hell.

"Perfect little athlete, huh?" Reagan muttered, his eyes narrowing in disgust. "Let's see how perfect you are when I'm done with you."

His heart raced with anticipation, each beat drumming out a promise of retribution. The thought of confronting Sheila, of making her pay for daring to involve herself in his plans, brought a sick sense of pleasure to the pit of his stomach. He could almost taste the fear and desperation that would soon drip from her every word, and the thought thrilled him.

Reagan glanced up at the darkened windows of Deirdre's dorm, his decision made. He would deal with Deirdre later—for now, he had a new target in his sights. With a determined stride, he stepped out of the shadows, ready to take control of the situation and face the woman who had dared to ensnare him.

CHAPTER TWENTY FOUR

Sheila's hands gripped the steering wheel as she pulled into the dark, deserted parking lot of the old steel mill. The headlights of her car cast eerie shadows on the cracked asphalt, and her heart pounded in her chest like a kickboxer's fists against a punching bag.

She scanned the area, searching for any signs of the person who called himself DarkReaper88, but there was nothing but darkness and silence. No other cars, no people, just the occasional rustle of leaves in the wind.

"You're ten minutes early," she whispered to herself, trying to calm her nerves. "You shouldn't be surprised he's not here yet."

The parking lot itself seemed to have been abandoned by time, its original purpose long forgotten. Weeds pushed their way through the cracks in the concrete, and an old railroad bridge loomed nearby, casting its skeletal shadow over the river below. In the distance, Sheila could hear the faint hum of traffic on the highway—a reminder that life continued on, oblivious to the danger she now faced.

A shiver ran down her spine as she considered the remoteness of this meeting place. It would be the perfect spot for the killer to strike, with no one around to hear her screams or come to her aid. Was that why he had chosen it? Did he intend to kill her here just because she had pretended to admire his gruesome handiwork?

"Stop it, Sheila," she scolded herself, shaking her head. "You're letting your fear get the best of you."

But the gnawing doubt in the pit of her stomach remained, making her question if she had made a monumental mistake in attempting to outsmart a man who was clearly very clever. Her ambition, the same drive that had propelled her to become an Olympic kickboxer and a Division 1 athlete, now felt like a liability.

For all her physical strength and intelligence, Sheila knew she couldn't rely on her fists or wits alone to survive this encounter. She was unarmed, and the killer – if he truly was coming – knew the terrain better than she did.

So why had she put herself in this position?

The sudden buzz of her phone startled Sheila, and she glanced down to see a text from Natalie: *Everything alright?*

She picked up the phone, her fingers hovering over the screen as she considered what to say. Telling Natalie where she was would only provoke a slew of questions, and almost certainly an instruction to wait for Natalie and Finn to back her up. Sheila couldn't do that, couldn't risk Natalie's safety that way, not after what had already happened.

You have to tell her something, she thought. *She'll get worried if you ignore her.*

Before she could think of how to respond, however, the sight of approaching headlights caught her attention.

"Damn it," Sheila muttered, dropping her phone onto the passenger seat and shielding her eyes with her arm. The brights were on, making it impossible to discern any details about the vehicle or its driver.

"Is that you?" she whispered, her heart pounding as adrenaline coursed through her veins. The vehicle continued to speed toward her, showing no sign of slowing down. Her instincts screamed at her, urging her to act.

Suddenly realizing what the driver intended to do, Sheila fumbled with her seat belt. Finally, it clicked open, and she flung the car door wide. She lunged out of the vehicle just as the truck slammed into her car with a deafening crash.

Sheila's racing heart pounded in her chest as she lay on the cold asphalt, her skinned knee throbbing mercilessly. The deafening crash of metal on metal still echoed in her ears, and the smell of gasoline filled her nostrils.

She rose on unsteady legs, watching as the large truck circled around like a shark circling a wounded whale. All she could do was watch, since she was unarmed and her only lifeline – her phone – lay trapped in the crumpled remains of the car.

The truck roared as it bore down on her again, its headlights cutting through the darkness like twin knives. Her mind raced, searching for an escape. Hiding behind her car would only prolong the inevitable—she'd be crushed if the killer rammed into it again. No, she needed another plan.

Sheila's gaze darted from the approaching truck to the clump of trees at the edge of the parking lot. Could she make it? They seemed so far away.

You'll never make it, she thought. *Long before you get there, he'll run you down.*

The truck roared, its engine a beast awakening from hibernation as it hurled toward Sheila. Panic clawed at her insides, but in the midst of her fear, a memory surfaced: Finn's flare gun in the glove box. It was her only chance.

"Sheila, you've got this," she whispered to herself, summoning every ounce of courage she possessed. She dove back into the wreckage of her car, fingers trembling as they fumbled with the jammed glove box. The roar of the truck's engine grew louder, each second an agonizing eternity.

"Come on, come on!" she said, frustration boiling over as the glove box latch refused to budge. Her heart hammered in her chest, threatening to burst free from its cage as the headlights of the truck grew brighter, engulfing the car in their unforgiving glare.

"Please, just open!" Sheila cried out, desperation lacing her voice.

With a final, determined pull, the glove box finally gave way, spilling its contents onto the floor. Her hand shot out, grasping the flare gun tightly, its cold metal a lifeline amidst the chaos. She noticed her phone lying nearby and snatched it up as well, unable to pass up such a crucial lifeline.

Scrambling from the car, Sheila steadied her aim at the oncoming truck, her vision blurred by sweat and tears. The monster of metal and horsepower bore down on her like a predator, closing in for the kill. But Sheila Stone was no prey; she was a fighter.

"Take this, you bastard!" she shouted, squeezing the trigger of the flare gun.

CHAPTER TWENTY FIVE

Sheila dove to the side, not wishing to be hit by the wrecked car should the truck plow into it. She landed hard on the buckled asphalt, and she felt dazed for a moment as she lifted her head to regard the truck.

The acrid smell of burnt rubber filled her nostrils as the truck's tires screeched against the asphalt. The flare, a violent dance of orange and red, cast an ominous glow upon the scene. Its brightness was almost blinding, but Sheila couldn't look away from the terrifying spectacle unfolding before her.

With a sickening crunch, the truck veered to the side, smashing headlong into the wrecked car. The impact shook the ground beneath Sheila's feet, jolting her back into awareness.

She waited for a few seconds, watching the truck to see if the driver would pull away or climb out. She could see no movement, however.

Sheila picked herself up off the cold ground, feeling her legs wobble beneath her. Her head throbbed, disoriented and dizzy from the sudden impact. She reached for the tender spot on the back of her head, wincing when her fingers brushed against a growing bump. She must've hit her head when she fell.

Bile rose in her throat, and for a moment she felt certain she'd be sick. Then the feeling passed, and she was steady again.

You can't keep having these close calls, she thought, *not with your injury history. One more good knock on the head, and it might be light's out—permanently.*

Squinting through the muted light, Sheila took in her surroundings. To her left lay her smashed car, an unrecognizable heap of metal. To her right, the killer's truck loomed like a predator in the shadows, its hood still ablaze with the flickering flare. The eerie silence only heightened her sense of unease.

"Where are you?" she murmured.

The flare's harsh light intensified Sheila's headache as she cautiously approached, her hand raised to shield her eyes. The shadows seemed to flee from the truck and the smashed car, leaving them exposed in an island of eerie illumination.

Suddenly she remembered her phone. She ought to call for help. The thought of being on the phone now, however, with the killer potentially lurking nearby, filled her with unease. She needed her hands free in case she had to defend herself.

I'll just make sure he's unconscious, she thought. *Then, I'll keep an eye on him while I make the call.*

As she neared the truck, however, she noticed the driver's door hanging open, revealing an empty seat.

"Where is he?" she muttered, her voice taut with tension. Her headache seemed to pulse in time with her pounding heart, a relentless drumbeat urging her forward.

Suddenly, footsteps sounded behind her, shattering the silence. Instinct took over as she spun around, just in time to see a small, heavyset man charging toward her, knife in hand. He must have been hiding behind the wrecked car, waiting for his moment to strike.

As he lunged at her, she sidestepped his attack and backpedaled to put distance between them.

"Think you can fool me?" he hissed, swiping with the knife. The cold steel cut through the air mere inches from Sheila's face, sending a shiver down her spine. "Sandra? You really didn't think I'd be able to figure out who you were?"

Her pulse quickened as she realized he had seen through her ruse. She had hoped that by adopting the persona of Sandra, a carefree and naïve woman, she could draw the killer out. But now, it seemed her plan had backfired.

"Where are the police, *Sandra*?" he taunted, a cruel smile playing on his lips. "You really thought you could handle me all by yourself, didn't you? Had to prove yourself to your big sister, is that it?"

The words shocked Sheila. How did he know about Natalie? How had he discovered her identity?

He smiled. "You didn't think I could figure out who you were? How stupid do you think I am?"

He thrust the knife forward, but Sheila dodged to the side. Despite the terror gripping her chest, she couldn't help but notice how unskilled the man was. His movements were clumsy, lacking the precision and finesse of a trained fighter. She felt a flicker of hope—without the element of surprise, perhaps he wasn't as dangerous as he appeared.

"Stupid enough," she muttered under her breath as she dodged another wild swipe. Her muscles tensed, ready to strike.

"What did you say?" he demanded.

"Stupid enough to underestimate me," she said. In one fluid motion, she blocked his next attack and delivered a powerful kick to his chest, sending him staggering backward. His eyes widened in shock, and for a moment, she saw fear in them—fear mixed with an undiluted hatred.

"If you know who I am," she continued, her words dripping with confidence, "then you must know I'm a former Olympic kickboxer. If you think a piece of pointy steel gives you the advantage, think again."

As she spoke, she studied his reaction, gauging whether her calculated display of strength had been enough to deter him. The man's face contorted with rage, and there was a hint of uncertainty in his eyes.

"Go on, then," she challenged, her heart pounding in her chest. "Let's see if you can really handle someone who knows how to fight back."

The hesitation in the man's eyes was palpable, as if he were weighing his options. Sheila held her breath, ready for his next move. And then, without warning, he spun on his heel and sprinted back toward the truck.

"Damn it!" Sheila cursed under her breath, breaking into a run after him. She couldn't let him escape, not now when she was so close to stopping him once and for all.

She expected the man to jump into the driver's seat, but instead, he yanked open the rear passenger door of the truck. Confused but still determined, Sheila closed the gap between them, her heart pounding in her ears.

As she neared the truck, she caught a glimpse of a figure bound and gagged in the back. The woman's eyes were wide with terror, her face pale and streaked with tears. Sheila's blood ran cold, and her resolve hardened—she couldn't let this monster hurt anyone else.

"Stop right there!" the man bellowed, pressing the knife to the captive woman's throat. His voice shook with a volatile blend of fear and rage. "Get one step closer, and I'll slit her throat!"

CHAPTER TWENTY SIX

Sheila's heart raced as she stared into the back of the truck, her breaths coming in short gasps. The dim glow from a nearby streetlight cast eerie shadows across the man's face as he pressed the knife to the throat of the college girl who was bound and gagged beside him.

He looked out of control, his eyes wild, his grip on the blade unsteady. Sheila had no doubt that he would kill the woman if she didn't do what he wanted.

She swallowed hard, fear tightening her chest. Once again, someone might get hurt because of her, just like Natalie had. The memory of her sister's injury weighed heavily on her conscience. She couldn't let it happen again.

"Hey," Sheila said, trying to keep her voice steady. "Let's just all calm down, okay? Why don't you tell me what you want."

The man's bloodshot eyes flicked toward her. His rage was palpable, and beneath it, she could see a deep-rooted pain. "I want some respect for once," he snarled. "I've been pushed around all my life, and I won't allow it anymore. Now *I'm* in control." He tightened his grip on the knife. "Now, others will do what *I* want."

"Yes, you're in control," Sheila said, careful not to do or say anything that might provoke him into harming the girl. "You have all the cards right now."

"That's right I do," he said, trying to smile. It was more of a grimace than a smile. "You think that just because you're athletic and know how to throw a punch that I should just surrender to you? You think that's the only kind of strength there is?"

"I know it isn't," she said. "And you're proving that right now."

He shook his head bitterly. "You know what they did to me? You know how they 'initiated' me into high school?"

Sheila waited. The man's voice was raw with emotion, and it was clear that whatever he was going to say was something he'd kept inside for a long time. He looked to be in his early forties, so whatever had happened to him back in high school, he must have been chewing on it for many years.

"So there was this pool party," he began. "All the popular kids were there, drinking and having a good time. I thought it was my chance to fit in, you know? To finally belong to a group." He shook his head, his lip curling in disdain.

"So there was this balcony," he continued. "The other kids thought it was fun to jump off it into the pool. I made the mistake of telling someone I was afraid of heights, and as soon as they heard that, they decided it was time to conquer my fear by jumping into the pool." He shuddered.

"Did you?" Sheila asked softly, aware of the girl's eyes staring at her, tense and silent.

The man nodded. "I did. Caught my foot on the edge, too, and ended up falling just short of the pool. You believe that? I broke my leg, and from then on, nobody wanted to talk to me. It was like I was an embarrassment, a bad memory."

He continued, anger simmering beneath his words. "Three surgeries later, my family went into huge debt. I think the stress is why my father had a heart attack. And all because of some stupid prank those assholes pulled."

Listening to him, Sheila felt a flicker of sympathy deep within her chest. She understood the need for validation, the desire to prove oneself after being knocked down time and time again. And yet, she knew she couldn't let that justify his current actions.

"Listen," she began gently, "I'm sorry that happened to you. No one should be bullied like that. But hurting her" – she glanced at the terrified college girl – "isn't going to make things right."

The man's eyes narrowed suddenly, and he stiffened. "You think I want your pity? You think I told you all that just so you'd feel bad for me?" He laughed. "Look at you, Miss Division One athlete. You think you can relate to me? You think you have any clue what I've been through?"

Sheila thought of mentioning what it was like to live in the shadow of a more successful older sister, but then she realized such a point wouldn't help her case. The truth was, she'd never been bullied the way this man had.

"You're as bad as all the rest," he said. "If you'd been at that party, you would have been one of the ones pushing me to jump. You and your friends, laughing at me for being scared. You don't know what it's like to be the outcast, to be the one everyone picks on."

Sheila took a deep breath, searching for the right words. "I may not know what it's like to be in your shoes, but I do know that hurting others isn't the answer. You have the power to break that cycle of pain and hurt, to rise above it and become something better. Don't let your anger control you."

The man's eyes softened momentarily, but then the anger flared again. He pointed the knife at her. "You're just saying that to get me to give up control. You just want me to lock away and throw the key. Sure, you act like you care now, but as soon as the tables are turned, you'll spit in my face."

Sheila started to protest, but before she could get far, the man said in a harsh voice, "I'm done talking with you. Shut up and start driving."

Sensing the man's volatility, Sheila knew she had no choice but to comply. She slid into the driver's seat of the damaged truck, her muscles tense and coiled like a spring. The keys were already in the ignition, waiting for her trembling hand to turn them.

"Drive," the man commanded, his knife still poised at the college girl's throat.

The engine roared to life, and Sheila shifted the truck into reverse to back away from the wrecked car. With one hand on the steering wheel, she surreptitiously reached into her pocket and pulled out her phone. Her fingers navigated the screen with practiced precision, texting Natalie.

In trouble. Man has a girl hostage. Driving now. Need help ASAP.

"Where am I going?" she asked through gritted teeth, trying to keep her voice steady.

"Take us to the old railroad bridge over the river," the man said.

"And then what?" she asked, a sense of foreboding building inside her.

"That's for me to know and you to find out later, sweetheart."

As they approached the dilapidated bridge, Sheila felt her heart sink. The once imposing structure now stood as a skeletal monument to its former glory. Its wooden beams were weathered and worn, their paint peeling away in long, mournful strips. Rust clung to the metal joints like a disease, eating away at the bridge's very foundation. The sight of it sent an involuntary shiver down her spine.

Sheila hesitated before turning onto the bridge, her eyes darting between the decaying structure and the man who held her and the girl captive. She couldn't afford to let her fear get the best of her; she had to focus on getting them all out of this alive. As her foot pressed down on the gas pedal, she silently prayed that the bridge would hold their weight just long enough for her to figure out what to do next.

As the truck rumbled onto the bridge, the old wooden planks creaked and groaned beneath them, voicing their objections to the unwelcome intrusion. Sheila's knuckles whitened around the steering wheel, her grip tightening as she fought to keep control of the truck and her rising panic. *Think, Sheila, think,* she urged herself, desperately searching for a way out of this nightmare.

The truck's tires rolled hesitantly over the ancient wooden planks, each one emitting a nerve-wracking groan beneath their weight. Sheila could practically feel the rotting wood straining, threatening to give way at any moment.

"Are you sure this is safe?" she asked. "It might not hold us."

"Drive!" the man barked, his eyes blazing with a dangerous fire. "I said drive!"

Swallowing hard, Sheila guided the truck deeper into the skeletal embrace of the decaying bridge. Her hands trembled on the wheel, cold sweat gathering on her brow. *Please, hold,* she silently begged the structure, her heart pounding like a drum against her ribcage.

As they reached the halfway point, the man raised his hand. "Stop," he commanded, his voice low and menacing. Sheila's foot pressed down on the brake pedal, bringing the truck to a shuddering halt.

"Get out," the man ordered, the knife still clutched tightly in his grip.

"Why?" Sheila asked, her gaze fixed on the glint of the blade, fear curdling in her stomach.

"Because," he snarled, his face contorted with rage, "you're going to jump, just like those bullies made me jump into that pool all those years ago. How's that for poetic justice?"

CHAPTER TWENTY SEVEN

Sheila's heart pounded in her chest as she stepped out of the truck, the cold metal handle leaving a momentary chill on her palm. The old, dilapidated railroad bridge creaked beneath her feet, its wooden boards showing the wear of time and weather. She could hear the water far below, its roar a constant reminder of the danger that lay beneath her. The drop was so far that she knew there was a good chance she would lose consciousness on the way down or when she hit the water. Her chances of survival would not be good.

Come on, she told herself. *You've faced worse odds in the boxing ring.* The difference, of course, was that the stakes here were far more serious, far more significant.

This wasn't about winning and losing—it was about life and death.

Taking a deep breath to steady herself, Sheila approached the edge of the bridge. The moon cast a silver glow over the rugged landscape, illuminating the mountains of Utah like otherworldly sentinels. Far below, the river churned, a dark ribbon slicing through the rocky terrain. It was late at night, and the stars twinkled overhead, their beauty contrasting sharply with the perilous situation she found herself in.

The wind whipped around her, ruffling her hair and tugging at her clothes as if it were a living thing trying to pull her away from the edge. She swallowed hard. As she stared down into the abyss, she knew that the next few moments would determine not only her fate but that of an innocent girl and perhaps others.

The truck's door slammed shut as the man stepped out, his menacing figure silhouetted against the moonlit sky. In one swift motion, he yanked his captive from the backseat, holding a knife to her trembling throat. Her eyes locked onto Sheila's, pleading for salvation.

"Everything's going to be okay," Sheila assured her.

"Not for you, sweetheart," the man sneered, his amusement palpable. "Not after you jump. There's no way you'll survive that fall."

Sheila's mind raced back to the text message she had sent Natalie. Had she seen it yet? When would help arrive? She knew she needed to buy time, and the only way to do so was to stroke this man's ego—not an easy feat, given his evident sadism.

"Fine," she said, her heart pounding in her chest. "But before I jump, tell me something. What will you do after this? You seem like a man with ambition."

The man's eyes narrowed, and for a moment, Sheila worried she had miscalculated. But then, his lips curled into a sinister grin. "Oh, I've got plans," he replied, never taking the blade away from the girl's throat. "Big plans."

"Like what?" she asked, trying to sound genuinely interested rather than desperate.

"Wouldn't you like to know?" the man taunted, clearly enjoying her discomfort.

"Maybe I would," Sheila said, injecting her voice with determination. "Or maybe I want others to know, too. To understand why you're doing this."

He arched an eyebrow. "Really? And why should I listen to a word you're saying?"

"Because I'm about to jump off this bridge for you," she said, hoping her gamble would pay off. "I think that earns me the right to know what I'm dying for."

The man considered this for a moment, then nodded. "You want the truth? Fine. After tonight, no one will forget my name. They'll know who I am and what I've done. And they'll respect it—or fear it."

"Then tell your story to the world," she urged, her heart pounding like a drumbeat in her ears. "Let them see the power you hold." She pulled out her phone and showed it to him. "I can record you right now—live-stream this, if you want. Otherwise, you're just wasting a perfect opportunity."

"And I suppose you want me to hold the phone, right? You're just going to hand it to me without trying any funny business?" He chuckled darkly. "No, I'm afraid I'm not that simple-minded."

Sheila's heart raced as she watched the man's grip tighten around the knife at his victim's throat.

"How many more people are on your list?" she asked. "How many do you plan to make pay for their actions?"

The man smirked, a twisted glint in his eyes. "There are more names, of course. The ones who stood by and did nothing while I was tormented—they're just as guilty as those who pushed me over the edge." His gaze turned steely. "It's only right that justice is served and they're punished for what they've done."

"Justice," Sheila murmured, trying to hide her disgust behind a facade of admiration. She needed him to believe she was on his side, even if it made her stomach churn. "You could really make a statement, you know. Have you considered speaking to a reporter? Sharing your story might inspire others to fight back against their own bullies."

He eyed her suspiciously, and she held her breath, praying he'd take the bait. "You think I should just hand myself over to the authorities? Is that it?"

"No, no," she assured him. "I meant what I said earlier. I find what you're doing...admirable. If you share your story, maybe more people will have the courage to stand up to their tormentors."

The man seemed intrigued by her suggestion, his grip on the knife loosening ever so slightly. "Maybe," he mused.

"Imagine the impact your message could have on a national stage," Sheila persisted, her voice steady despite the fear clawing at her insides. "You'd be giving a voice to all those who've been silenced by bullies."

The man seemed to consider her words, his expression shifting like quicksilver as he weighed the possibilities. She could see the allure of fame and recognition in his eyes, and she pressed her advantage. "You'd reach millions of people, make them understand why you're doing this. They'd see that you're not just some mindless killer but a man with a cause."

"National TV, huh?" He tilted his head, the knife still dangerously close to his hostage's throat. "I could make them all listen...make them all pay attention."

"Exactly," she said, her heart pounding faster as she sensed him wavering. "You'd become more than just a name in the headlines. You'd be someone they couldn't ignore. A legend."

His gaze froze. All at once, Sheila realized she'd made a mistake, tried too hard to sell the ruse.

The man's eyes narrowed, and he sneered in contempt. "You think I'm an idiot? You're just stalling, trying to save your own skin." He tightened his grip on the knife, pressing it against the trembling girl's throat. "You don't care about my cause. Admit it!"

"No, I..." Sheila stuttered, but her voice failed her as the panic surged through her veins. She had come so close to winning him over, but now her desperation was laid bare.

"Jump!" he snarled, his patience clearly at its end. "Or she dies."

Sheila hesitated for a moment, searching for another way out, but there were no other options left. With a heavy heart, she took a step toward the edge of the bridge, her boots crunching on the gravel. The wind roared around her as she peered down into the inky darkness, the river below a cold, unforgiving abyss.

Her thoughts turned to Natalie as she teetered precariously on the edge of oblivion. Would this sacrifice be enough to make amends for the pain she'd caused her sister? Or would it all be for nothing, leaving the man free to continue his bloody rampage?

"Three seconds, Miss Stone!" the man said, his voice echoing through the dark expanse. "One!"

Sheila's breath came in ragged gasps as she desperately searched for any other option. She clenched her fists, nails digging into her palms as she tried to steady herself.

"Two!"

Time seemed to slow as the wind whipped around her, tangling her hair and tugging at her clothes. She could feel the rough, weathered wood beneath her feet, the damp chill of the night air clinging to her skin. Her mind raced, drawing on every ounce of her Olympic training and experience, but it all felt futile in the face of this impossible choice.

"Thr—"

"Wait!" she cried out, her voice choked with fear and desperation. But her plea fell on deaf ears as the man raised the knife, its blade gleaming menacingly in the faint moonlight.

Sheila's heart ached for the girl who stood trembling beside her tormentor. The girl's eyes were wide with terror, tears streaming down her face. She didn't deserve this fate.

Sheila knew there was only one thing left to do. Summoning every ounce of strength and courage she possessed, she closed her eyes.

And then she leaped into the abyss.

CHAPTER TWENTY EIGHT

As Sheila plummeted toward the dark abyss below, her instincts kicked in, and she reached out desperately. Her fingers brushed against something cold and metallic—a frayed cable that had once been part of the bridge's structure. Rusty and forgotten, it dangled precariously from the crumbling framework.

She grabbed hold of the cable and felt a jarring ache in her shoulders as her body came to an abrupt stop. She clung desperately to the cable, scarcely able to believe she was still alive, her mind entirely focused on how to make sure her fingers didn't slip.

Against her better judgment, she found herself stealing a glimpse down at the water churning far below. Moonlight glinted off the white water, hinting at the presence of hidden stones.

You've done the hard part, she told herself. *Now, all you have to do is pull yourself back up.*

She forced herself to take slow, deep breaths. As her grip tightened around the cable, she strained to listen for any sounds above. A few of the boards creaked, and she imagined the man leading his captive back into his truck, ready perhaps to take her to whatever locker he intended to be her coffin.

Sheila, however, could not let that happen. Once again, he'd underestimated her, assuming there was no way she could come back. And once again, she would prove him wrong.

With her determination ignited, Sheila began the arduous ascent. The cable bit into her palms, the rust scraping away at her skin, but she refused to let go. She gritted her teeth and focused on the rhythm of her breaths, each inhale and exhale a testament to her unwavering resolve.

Come on, Sheila, she thought, *you've got this.*

Her muscles quivered with exertion as she pulled herself upward, inch by agonizing inch. Her years of training as an Olympic athlete had prepared her for physical challenges, but nothing could have prepared her for the life-or-death stakes of this moment. Sweat trickled down her face, mixing with the blood from her torn hands, yet she pushed on.

As Sheila neared the top of the bridge, the distant sounds of voices and the flickering glow of a flashlight caught her attention. Her pulse quickened, hope surging through her veins like wildfire.

Help is here, she thought. *I just need to make it to the top.*

With one final Herculean effort, Sheila hoisted herself onto the bridge. Exhaustion wracked her body, but she forced herself to keep moving. The cold wood beneath her scraped against her skin, but the sensation was welcome compared to the fear of falling that had gripped her moments before.

Then she heard it—a voice she would have recognized anywhere. Natalie's commanding tone cut through the night air, bringing Sheila equal parts relief and trepidation.

"Drop the knife!" Natalie shouted, her words laced with urgency.

Sheila glanced up to see her sister and Finn parked at the end of the bridge, their weapons drawn and aimed at the man who had forced her to jump from the bridge. He stood mere feet away from her, his victim trembling in his grasp as he pressed the knife to her throat. The man's truck idled nearby, its headlights casting eerie shadows across the desolate scene.

Damn it, Sheila thought, her heart pounding in her chest. *If he realizes he's trapped, he'll kill the girl for sure.*

In that instant, the weight of her responsibility settled on her like a thousand-pound anchor. She knew she had to act fast.

She rose to her feet, the adrenaline coursing through her veins. She focused on each slow, deliberate step she took toward the man, every muscle in her body tensed and ready. A bead of sweat trickled down her temple as she listened to the man shout at Natalie and Finn.

"Stay back," he warned, his voice shaking with desperation. "I swear I'll kill her!"

"Drop the knife!" Natalie said again, her tone unwavering.

For a moment, time seemed to stand still. The man hesitated, glancing between the girl in his grasp and the two officers with their weapons trained on him. Then, as if giving up, he let the knife slip from his fingers. It clattered to the wooden planks and disappeared through a gap, swallowed by the darkness below.

"Good," Natalie said, her voice hard but relieved. "Now let her go."

"Let her go?" he repeated softly, then let out a dry chuckle. "Oh, she'll go, alright."

With that, the man gave the girl a violent shove toward the edge of the bridge. Sheila's breath caught in her throat as she saw the girl teetering precariously over the abyss.

"NO!" she screamed, lunging forward.

Her fingers wrapped around the girl's wrist just as she began to topple over the edge. Sheila sank to the floor, stretched out on her belly, her grip on the girl the only thing keeping her from plummeting to her death.

"Help me!" the girl cried, terror etched across her face.

"Hold on," Sheila said through clenched teeth, her muscles strained to their limit. "I've got you."

Behind her, she heard the man curse as he raced toward them, his footsteps heavy on the creaking bridge.

"You just can't stop interfering, can you?" he demanded, grabbing her leg and lifting her. He seemed to be intent on shoving her over the side of the bridge along with the girl. Two for the price of one, perhaps.

Sheila kicked out with her free leg, her foot connecting with the man's stomach and causing him to stagger backward. His face twisted with rage, and he came forward again. This time, he seized both of her legs and began to lift her, tipping her toward the edge of the bridge as she desperately tried to escape his grasp. Within seconds, the weight of the girl dangling above the water far below would prove too much, and then she and Sheila both would go plunging into the abyss.

Then, just as Sheila felt herself sliding along the boards, Finn slammed into the man, tackling him to the ground. They rolled several times before Finn came out on top, punching the man twice until he stopped fighting.

"Sheila!" Natalie shouted. "Hang in there!"

Sheila's arms burned with the effort as she fought to maintain her grip, every fiber of her being focused on the girl whose life hung in the balance. She knew that if she failed now, the guilt would haunt her forever.

The girl's eyes, wide with terror, locked onto Sheila's as she stared up at her would-be savior. "Please," she whimpered, tears streaming down her cheeks. "Don't let go."

"I won't," Sheila promised, barely able to get the words out, so great was the strain of her effort. "Just...hold...on."

Sheila's fingers slipped a fraction of an inch further, her sweat-slicked palms betraying her. She fought the urge to scream in frustration, focusing instead on her breathing.

Inhale, exhale. Just like you were trained to do—find your center, harness your power.

"Help me!" the girl cried, her voice cracking under the strain.

"Stay calm," Sheila whispered through clenched teeth, her mind racing. Finn was busy pinning the knife-wielding maniac to the ground, and Natalie – strong, capable Natalie – couldn't move from her wheelchair to assist. It was all on Sheila.

"Sheila," Natalie called out, anxiety lacing her words. "You can do this!"

Gritting her teeth, Sheila summoned every ounce of strength she had left. She pulled her legs up until she was in a kneeling position. Then she leaned back, slipping her legs forward and digging her heels into the splintered wood of the bridge. Every muscle in her body screamed in protest as she pulled on the girl's arm, inch by agonizing inch.

"Come on," she said with a grunt, her vision blurring as pain pulsed through her skull. "We're not dying here. Not today."

Her arms trembled with the effort, but she refused to yield. She had already lost so much; she wouldn't let this girl slip through her fingers too.

With a final, Herculean effort, Sheila hauled the girl up and over the edge of the bridge. They collapsed onto the wooden planks, their breaths coming in ragged gasps.

"Thank you," the girl whispered, her voice trembling with relief as she clung to Sheila's arm.

Sheila lay there, her body battered and exhausted, but alive. She had done it—alone and against all odds. And for the first time in a long while, she felt something other than the crushing weight of failure: she felt hope.

The chilling wind cut through Sheila's sweat-drenched clothes, making her shiver as she lay on the worn wooden planks of the bridge. The girl she had just saved huddled close to her, tears streaming down her face.

"Hey," Sheila whispered, trying to sound reassuring despite her own exhaustion, "you're safe now."

"Thank you," the girl managed to say, her voice weak and shaky.

As they lay there, the soft sound of wheels against wood approached. Natalie rolled up beside Sheila, her eyes filled with a mixture of concern and respect. She locked the brakes on her wheelchair and leaned forward slightly, scanning her sister's body for any signs of injury.

"Sheila," Natalie said softly, "I'm so proud of you."

Sheila blinked back tears, surprised by the warmth that flooded her at her sister's words. It was rare for Natalie to express her feelings openly, especially when it came to their turbulent relationship.

"Thanks, Nat," she said, her voice cracking. She knew the gravity of what she had just done—faced the fear of failure and emerged triumphant.

Natalie glanced over at the girl Sheila had saved, her protective instincts kicking in. "Are you alright?" she asked, concern evident in her voice.

The girl nodded, wiping away tears with a trembling hand. "Yes, thanks to her."

CHAPTER TWENTY NINE

Sheila winced as she massaged her aching shoulder, the pain a constant reminder of the ordeal she had just gone through. The adrenaline rush had begun to subside, leaving her muscles tense and sore, but the satisfaction of success far outweighed the discomfort. She couldn't help but feel a surge of pride knowing she'd helped save a life.

The dilapidated old railroad bridge loomed overhead, its rusting metal frame casting eerie shadows on the ground below. Sheila, Natalie, and Finn stood at the edge, bathed in the faint glow of the pre-dawn sky. A cacophony of sirens filled the air as police cars and ambulances clustered nearby, their flashing lights cutting through the darkness.

"Are you sure you're alright, Sheila?" Natalie asked, concern etched on her face as she studied her younger sister.

"Yeah, I'm fine," Sheila assured her, forcing a smile to mask her lingering pain. "Just a little sore."

Natalie frowned but didn't push further. Instead, her gaze followed Sheila's to the scene unfolding before them. The college girl they had saved was sitting on the back bumper of an ambulance, wrapped in a thermal blanket as a medic checked her vital signs. Her eyes darted nervously around, still trying to process the nightmare she had just escaped.

A short distance away, the killer – his face twisted with anger and defeat – was being roughly ushered into the back of a police car. His hands were cuffed behind his back, and two officers flanked him, making sure he didn't try anything desperate. As the door slammed shut, Sheila felt a chill crawl up her spine—that man could have easily become the last person she saw alive if she hadn't been careful.

Amidst the chaos of flashing lights and bustling emergency personnel, Sheila took a deep breath and savored the metallic scent of the crisp night air. Her heart still hammered in her chest from the adrenaline, but as she glanced at Natalie and Finn, she felt an overwhelming sense of accomplishment.

"I'm still trying to piece everything together," Natalie said, looking puzzled. "What happened? How did you know to find him here?"

Sheila hesitated for a moment, replaying the events in her mind. "Well, I just got the sense that Kyle Benedict wasn't the type of person to physically attack someone else—he seemed more like the kind to attack them anonymously and stop there. So I went back to his blog, trying to see if I was missing something, and I came across some really hateful comments someone else had written about the victims, even threatening to harm them."

She swallowed hard before continuing. "I reached out to this person, and he...well, he sort of hinted that he was the one who'd killed them. He invited me to meet with him, said I could 'pick his brain,' so I agreed."

Natalie shook her head, looking troubled. "You could've gotten yourself killed, Sheila. We might never have known what happened to you."

Finn chimed in, a proud smile stretching across his face. "But she didn't, Nat. She did great police work, even if it wasn't exactly by-the-book." He slapped Sheila on the shoulder, making her wince slightly. "The bottom line is about getting results, and she did just that."

Sheila felt warmth spread through her chest as Finn's words settled in. She knew her methods hadn't been conventional, but the outcome spoke for itself. And with Natalie and Finn standing beside her, she felt invincible. They were a team, and together, they had managed to bring a killer to justice.

"Thanks, Finn," she murmured, her gaze flickering between her sister and the deputy. "I couldn't have done it without both of you."

Natalie's gaze softened as she took in Finn's praise of Sheila. "Alright, point made," she said with a small smile. "In fact, I think it's time for you to officially become a police officer."

Sheila blinked in surprise, her heart skipping a beat. "Are you sure?" she asked cautiously.

"Of course. You'll have to go through training, but I think you'd be great for the job. Besides, it would make Dad proud." Her eyes held a hint of sadness, and Sheila couldn't help but think it was because Natalie, now confined to a wheelchair, wasn't the cop she used to be anymore.

Before Sheila could respond to the invitation, the college girl they had rescued approached them nervously, her eyes filled with gratitude. "I...I just wanted to thank you," she stammered, looking at Sheila. "You saved my life."

Sheila felt a rush of humility and gestured to Natalie and Finn. "It wasn't just me. These two did just as much to save you."

The girl smiled, tears brimming in her eyes. "Thank you, all of you," she said, her voice wavering with emotion.

"What's your name?" Finn asked gently.

"Brooke Fowler," she said, wiping away a stray tear.

"Nice to meet you, Brooke. I'm Finn, this is Sheila, and that's Natalie," he said, introducing the trio.

A vehicle pulled up a short distance away, and for a brief moment, the headlights fell on Sheila's face, casting stark shadows across her cheeks. A man and a woman got out, their expressions etched with concern as they scanned the scene. Brooke's gaze followed theirs, and her eyes widened with recognition.

"Those are my parents," she whispered, her voice wavering.

"Go to them," Sheila said, her heart swelling with empathy for the family reunion unfolding before her. "They must be worried sick."

"Thank you," Brooke said again, looking from Sheila to Natalie and Finn. "I don't know how I'll ever repay you." With that, she hurried over to her parents, who enveloped her in a desperate embrace. The sight of their relief made Sheila grateful for their small victory in the larger battle against crime.

As the Fowlers shared their tearful reunion, Natalie turned back to Sheila, her wheelchair humming softly as it pivoted. "So, about becoming a police officer... Take some time to think it over, okay?" Her eyes searched Sheila's face for any signs of doubt.

But Sheila didn't need time. She had found new purpose in this line of work, and the thought of saving lives and making a real difference in the world filled her with determination. "I don't need to think about it," she said, her voice steady and resolute. "I want to become a cop."

Natalie's eyes widened, but then a proud smile spread across her face. "You're sure?"

"Absolutely," Sheila said, and she could feel Finn's approving gaze on her as well. As his hand landed on her shoulder, he gave her an encouraging nod. The sense of validation warmed her from within, and she knew without a doubt that she was on the right path.

"Alright, Sheila," Natalie said, her voice softening. "We'll start the process as soon as possible."

"Thank you," Sheila replied, and she meant it with every fiber of her being. The moment was bittersweet, but she knew that this was the beginning of something important, not just for her but for everyone whose lives she would touch along the way.

Natalie maneuvered her wheelchair expertly, the faint whir of its motor blending with the distant sounds of the authorities still working at the scene. "I'm heading home to get some rest," she said, casting a concerned glance at Sheila. "You should do the same."

"Rest would be great," Sheila agreed, but there was one question that still nagged at her. "But who was the murderer?"

Finn crossed his arms and sighed. "As of now, all we know is what we've learned from the contents of his wallet. His name is John Reagan Dreyer. He was a student at Coldwater Community College, but he was in an internship program that led him to visit other local campuses, including Clearview University and Elbridge College, where the bodies of the other two victims were found. That was how he was able to visit the other campuses without arousing suspicion." He shook his head. "I don't know why Dreyer murdered those girls, though."

Sheila closed her eyes for a moment, recalling the desperate look in Dreyer's eyes as he'd revealed his motives to her. "I know why," she said. "He told me about how he'd been bullied by the victims – and others – at a party. They forced him to jump from a balcony into a pool." She paused, the memory unsettling. "The problem was that he stumbled and landed on concrete, breaking his leg. He never stopped wanting revenge for that."

Natalie's expression softened, and she looked away, her fingers tightening around the wheels of her chair. "I understand what it's like to be bitter over such an injury," she murmured, "but that doesn't give anyone the right to resort to violence."

Sheila watched her sister, her heart aching at the reminder of the pain Natalie had endured. She wanted to reach out, to offer comfort, but she knew that words would never be enough to heal the wounds they both shared. Instead, she focused on the glimmer of hope that had been ignited within her—the opportunity to make a difference in this world.

"Sometimes," Sheila said softly, "the monsters we face are created by our own hands."

Finn took a deep breath and let it out slowly. "I'd toast to that, if I could. Well, Nat, what do you say I get you both home? It's been a long day."

Natalie nodded, stifling a yawn. "I'm on board with that plan."

The night air was heavy with the scent of damp earth and gasoline as they made their way toward the van, the flashing lights from the emergency vehicles casting surreal shadows on the ground. Sheila could feel her muscles tense and relax with each step, the adrenaline slowly leaving her body after the intense confrontation with Dreyer.

"Y'know," Finn said, breaking the silence between them, "I'm going to have a hard time forgiving you for wrecking my car."

Sheila shot him a sidelong glance, a hint of amusement in her eyes. "Last I checked, it was Dreyer who totaled your car, not me."

Finn huffed, feigning annoyance, but the corners of his mouth twitched upward. "Oh, sure. Blame it on the crazy sociopath. How convenient."

They shared a laugh, the tension easing further from their bodies. It felt good to find humor in the midst of such darkness.

Riding this wave of good feelings, Sheila decided to ask Finn a question that had been on her mind for a while now. "What's the deal with the necklace?" she asked. "I couldn't help noticing it earlier. I'm not trying to be pushy, I'm just—"

"Curious?" He arched an eyebrow.

She nodded. "That's right. I can tell it's important to you."

Finn glanced at Natalie, who had moved on ahead of them, speeding along in her wheelchair. He sighed, sounding suddenly weary. "It's a long story," he said, "and it's very late to begin a long story."

Sheila said nothing for several heartbeats. It was indeed late, but she sensed that there was no telling when he might be willing to open up again. She wanted to strike while the iron was hot.

"Give me the cliff notes, then," she said. "Where'd you get it?"

He stared ahead, his eyes solemn. "It was in my survival gear back when I was flying F-35s."

Sheila waited. When she realized he wasn't going to volunteer anything more, she asked, "And is that why it's significant to you? Just because you had it when you were a fighter pilot?"

"Just?"

"I'm not trying to say it's insignificant." She paused, gathering her words. "I'm just wondering if there's something more to it. I don't see you still wearing your pilot's helmet around."

The remark seemed to catch Finn by surprise, and he laughed. "Fair enough." Growing serious again, he reached into his shirt and pulled out the compass. "This little guy saved my life. That's why I hold onto it. It reminds me of what almost happened…and what I almost did."

The words puzzled Sheila. Just then, however, her phone buzzed in her pocket, the vibration startling her.

"Don't you think you should get that?" Finn asked.

She hesitated. "Yes, but I want to hear what you have to say. What almost happened? What did you almost do?"

He smiled sadly and waved a dismissive hand. "Another time, Sheila. Like I said, it's a long story."

They had reached the van. Natalie was already inside, and now Finn climbed in. It was clear to Sheila that they weren't going to be able to continue their conversation. As curious as she was to hear what Finn had meant, she needed to respect his boundaries.

Before joining Finn and Natalie in the van, Sheila pulled out her phone and looked at the screen. She had a new voicemail from her father. She remembered he had texted her earlier about having dinner together, but this message seemed more urgent.

Sheila, call me as soon as you can. There's something very important I'd like to speak with you about—something we should keep between the two of us, at least for now.

"You coming?" Natalie called out the window.

"Just give me a moment," she said as she tried to make sense of her father's words.

Natalie hesitated, her gaze searching Sheila's face for any sign of distress. "Is everything okay?"

"Everything's fine," Sheila reassured her, keeping her father's request for secrecy in mind. "Actually, why don't you two go on without me? I'll ask one of the other officers to drive me home."

"Are you sure?" Finn asked, concern etched in the lines around his eyes.

"Positive," she said. She did her best to offer a reassuring smile.

With a nod and a wave, Finn and Natalie drove off, leaving Sheila alone with her thoughts and the urgent message from her father. The weight of his words settled upon her shoulders as she stood at the edge of the bridge, her heart pounding.

What, she wondered, could her father need to tell her so badly?

EPILOGUE

Sheila paced along the edge of the dilapidated bridge, waiting for her father to pick up the phone.

"Come on, Dad...pick up," she muttered under her breath, her fingers tapping an impatient rhythm on her thigh. She had called him back just a few minutes after he'd called her, so why wasn't he answering—especially if this was 'very important'?

The early morning air was cool against her skin, and the scent of damp earth filled her nostrils. Her breath formed small clouds in the gradually lightening sky. It was hard to believe that she had nearly fallen from this bridge less than an hour earlier.

Finally, Gabriel Stone's voice came through the line, sounding gruff and serious. "Sheila, thanks for calling me back."

"Of course, Dad," she replied, her voice tense with worry. "What's going on? You sounded really serious in your voicemail."

"Are you sitting down?" he asked.

"Is it Jason?" Sheila asked, fear gripping her chest tightly. "Did something happen to him?"

"No, no, it's not that," Gabriel reassured her, but his cryptic manner only served to heighten her anxiety. "I just need to talk to you about something important."

"Would you please just spit it out? This suspense is killing me."

There was a heavy sigh on the other end of the line before Gabriel finally spoke, his voice low and contemplative. "You know how I've spent my free time painting lately?"

"Yeah," she said cautiously, unsure where he was going with this.

"Well, that's not the only thing I've been doing. I've also been working on Henrietta's murder investigation."

Sheila's heart skipped a beat, her mind reeling from the revelation. Memories of her mother flooded her thoughts, leaving her momentarily breathless. "You...what? But why didn't you tell us?"

"I didn't want to give you false hope, make you feel like there was any guarantee of figuring out who killed her."

Sheila was silent for a few moments, thinking over the implications of what her father was saying. "But now you're bringing it up, which tells me there's been a development, right?"

Her father hesitated for a moment, clearly weighing his words. "I can't say for certain yet, but I think I might be onto something. It's not a guarantee, Sheila, but it's a start."

As she processed her father's words, Sheila felt a mixture of emotions welling up inside her: hope, fear, and a fierce determination to uncover the truth behind her mother's death.

"I haven't told Natalie, though," he added.

"Wait, why not?" Sheila asked, her eyebrows knitting together in confusion.

Gabriel hesitated before explaining. "I was going to, but then there was the shooting and all, and Nat..." He paused and sighed. "She's still recovering from what happened—not just physically, but emotionally as well. She needs time to adjust to the change, and bringing up her mother's death…" He took a deep breath and let it out slowly. "It would only put more strain on her."

"Don't you think she'd want to know? Don't you think she'll be angry with us later for not telling us?"

Gabriel's voice was grim. "That's certainly a possibility. She'll want to throw herself into this, do everything she can to figure out what happened—which is exactly why now is not the right time for her. She needs to recover, not obsess over a cold case, especially one so personal to her."

Sheila said nothing. She didn't like the idea of keeping Natalie in the dark.

"It's my decision, okay?" her father said. "I've made the call, and I'm just asking you to honor it. If later on she's upset about it, you can blame me."

"Okay, Dad," Sheila finally said. "I don't like it…but I understand."

"I know it sucks. But think about how it would feel to tell her we'd found Mom's killer, knowing we'd spared Nat the torture of dwelling on the uncertainty. Think about the way Nat's face would light up."

Sheila's voice was low, barely more than a whisper. "I can't tell you how much I want that."

"I know, Sheila. I know."

The conversation fell silent for a moment as Sheila's mind wandered to memories of her mother. She recalled how Henrietta would gently brush her hair after a long day of sparring, her tender touch soothing Sheila's tired muscles. She remembered the way her mother's laughter sounded, light and musical, filling their home with warmth and love. And she could still see the unwavering pride that shone in her mother's eyes every time she watched her daughters compete.

Tears threatened to spill from Sheila's eyes as she clutched her phone tightly, her knuckles turning white. This lead, however tentative it may be, could bring her a step closer to finding her mother's murderer, something she had long ago concluded might never happen.

"Okay, Dad," she said, her voice thick with emotion. "What's the lead? What have you found?"

There was a pause on the line, and she could almost hear her father weighing his words, calculating just how much he should reveal.

"I think I might've found the getaway vehicle," he said.

NOW AVAILABLE!

SILENT NIGHT
(A Sheila Stone Suspense Thriller—Book Three)

With a career-ending injury, Olympic kickboxer Sheila Stone is forced back to her small hometown, where her older sister, the local sheriff, offers her a spot on the local police force. When a body appears in Great Salt Lake, it sends shockwaves through the quiet community, and Sheila must draw on her fighting skills in a deadly race to save the next victim in time….

"A masterpiece of thriller and mystery."
—Books and Movie Reviews, Roberto Mattos (re Once Gone)

SILENT NIGHT (A Sheila Stone Suspense Thriller—Book 3) is Book #3 in a long-anticipated new series by #1 bestseller and USA Today bestselling author Blake Pierce, whose bestseller *The Perfect Wife* (a free download) has received over 20,000 five star reviews.

With her Olympic dreams crumbled, Sheila, 28, struggles to find her place back home. She is surrounded by reminders of what could have been, stuck inside the shadow of her older sister: the golden child, the respected sheriff. But when her sister persuades her to join the local police force, Sheila's life and career start anew.

As she hunts serial killers, Sheila notices clues that others miss and offers a perspective that no one else has. She realizes she has a talent outside of fighting, and that she has a chance to embrace a new life in Salt Lake—a life outside the ring.

This is a different kind of ring, though. Sheila quickly realizes that to survive, she will need more than just her strength—she'll need a brilliance to match that of even the most diabolical killer….

Can Sheila win this match? Or will she finally lose it all?

A page-turning and harrowing suspense thriller featuring a brilliant and tortured protagonist, the SHEILA STONE series is a riveting mystery, packed with suspense, twists and turns, revelations, and driven by a breakneck pace that will keep you flipping pages late into the night.

Future books in the series are also available.

"An edge of your seat thriller in a new series that keeps you turning pages! ...So many twists, turns and red herrings… I can't wait to see what happens next."
—Reader review (Her Last Wish)

"A strong, complex story about two FBI agents trying to stop a serial killer. If you want an author to capture your attention and have you guessing, yet trying to put the pieces together, Pierce is your author!"
—Reader review (Her Last Wish)

"A typical Blake Pierce twisting, turning, roller coaster ride suspense thriller. Will have you turning the pages to the last sentence of the last chapter!!!"
—Reader review (City of Prey)

"Right from the start we have an unusual protagonist that I haven't seen done in this genre before. The action is nonstop… A very atmospheric novel that will keep you turning pages well into the wee hours."
—Reader review (City of Prey)

"Everything that I look for in a book… a great plot, interesting characters, and grabs your interest right away. The book moves along at a breakneck pace and stays that way until the end. Now on go I to book two!"
—Reader review (Girl, Alone)

"Exciting, heart pounding, edge of your seat book… a must read for mystery and suspense readers!"
—Reader review (Girl, Alone)

Blake Pierce

Blake Pierce is the USA Today bestselling author of the RILEY PAGE mystery series, which includes seventeen books. Blake Pierce is also the author of the MACKENZIE WHITE mystery series, comprising fourteen books; of the AVERY BLACK mystery series, comprising six books; of the KERI LOCKE mystery series, comprising five books; of the MAKING OF RILEY PAIGE mystery series, comprising six books; of the KATE WISE mystery series, comprising seven books; of the CHLOE FINE psychological suspense mystery, comprising six books; of the JESSIE HUNT psychological suspense thriller series, comprising thirty-five books (and counting); of the AU PAIR psychological suspense thriller series, comprising three books; of the ZOE PRIME mystery series, comprising six books; of the ADELE SHARP mystery series, comprising sixteen books, of the EUROPEAN VOYAGE cozy mystery series, comprising six books; of the LAURA FROST FBI suspense thriller, comprising eleven books; of the ELLA DARK FBI suspense thriller, comprising twenty-one books (and counting); of the A YEAR IN EUROPE cozy mystery series, comprising nine books, of the AVA GOLD mystery series, comprising six books; of the RACHEL GIFT mystery series, comprising thirteen books (and counting); of the VALERIE LAW mystery series, comprising nine books; of the PAIGE KING mystery series, comprising eight books; of the MAY MOORE mystery series, comprising eleven books; of the CORA SHIELDS mystery series, comprising eight books; of the NICKY LYONS mystery series, comprising eight books, of the CAMI LARK mystery series, comprising ten books; of the AMBER YOUNG mystery series, comprising seven books (and counting); of the DAISY FORTUNE mystery series, comprising five books; of the FIONA RED mystery series, comprising eleven books (and counting); of the FAITH BOLD mystery series, comprising eleven books (and counting); of the JULIETTE HART mystery series, comprising five books (and counting); of the MORGAN CROSS mystery series, comprising nine books (and counting); of the FINN WRIGHT mystery series, comprising five books (and counting); of the new SHEILA STONE suspense thriller series, comprising five books (and counting); and of the new RACHEL BLACKWOOD suspense thriller series, comprising five books (and counting).

An avid reader and lifelong fan of the mystery and thriller genres, Blake loves to hear from you, so please feel free to visit www.blakepierceauthor.com to learn more and stay in touch.

BOOKS BY BLAKE PIERCE

RACHEL BLACKWOOD SUSPENSE THRILLER
NOT THIS WAY (Book #1)
NOT THIS TIME (Book #2)
NOT THIS CLOSE (Book #3)
NOT THIS ROAD (Book #4)
NOT THIS LATE (Book #5)

SHEILA STONE SUSPENSE THRILLER
SILENT GIRL (Book #1)
SILENT TRAIL (Book #2)
SILENT NIGHT (Book #3)
SILENT HOUSE (Book #4)
SILENT SCREAM (Book #5)

FINN WRIGHT MYSTERY SERIES
WHEN YOU'RE MINE (Book #1)
WHEN YOU'RE SAFE (Book #2)
WHEN YOU'RE CLOSE (Book #3)
WHEN YOU'RE SLEEPING (Book #4)
WHEN YOU'RE SANE (Book #5)

MORGAN CROSS MYSTERY SERIES
FOR YOU (Book #1)
FOR RAGE (Book #2)
FOR LUST (Book #3)
FOR WRATH (Book #4)
FOREVER (Book #5)
FOR US (Book #6)
FOR NOW (Book #7)
FOR ONCE (Book #8)
FOR ETERNITY (Book #9)

JULIETTE HART MYSTERY SERIES
NOTHING TO FEAR (Book #1)
NOTHING THERE (Book #2)

NOTHING WATCHING (Book #3)
NOTHING HIDING (Book #4)
NOTHING LEFT (Book #5)

FAITH BOLD MYSTERY SERIES

SO LONG (Book #1)
SO COLD (Book #2)
SO SCARED (Book #3)
SO NORMAL (Book #4)
SO FAR GONE (Book #5)
SO LOST (Book #6)
SO ALONE (Book #7)
SO FORGOTTEN (Book #8)
SO INSANE (Book #9)
SO SMITTEN (Book #10)
SO SIMPLE (Book #11)

FIONA RED MYSTERY SERIES

LET HER GO (Book #1)
LET HER BE (Book #2)
LET HER HOPE (Book #3)
LET HER WISH (Book #4)
LET HER LIVE (Book #5)
LET HER RUN (Book #6)
LET HER HIDE (Book #7)
LET HER BELIEVE (Book #8)
LET HER FORGET (Book #9)
LET HER TRY (Book #10)
LET HER PLAY (Book #11)

DAISY FORTUNE MYSTERY SERIES

NEED YOU (Book #1)
CLAIM YOU (Book #2)
CRAVE YOU (Book #3)
CHOOSE YOU (Book #4)
CHASE YOU (Book #5)

AMBER YOUNG MYSTERY SERIES

ABSENT PITY (Book #1)
ABSENT REMORSE (Book #2)

ABSENT FEELING (Book #3)
ABSENT MERCY (Book #4)
ABSENT REASON (Book #5)
ABSENT SANITY (Book #6)
ABSENT LIFE (Book #7)

CAMI LARK MYSTERY SERIES
JUST ME (Book #1)
JUST OUTSIDE (Book #2)
JUST RIGHT (Book #3)
JUST FORGET (Book #4)
JUST ONCE (Book #5)
JUST HIDE (Book #6)
JUST NOW (Book #7)
JUST HOPE (Book #8)
JUST LEAVE (Book #9)
JUST TONIGHT (Book #10)

NICKY LYONS MYSTERY SERIES
ALL MINE (Book #1)
ALL HIS (Book #2)
ALL HE SEES (Book #3)
ALL ALONE (Book #4)
ALL FOR ONE (Book #5)
ALL HE TAKES (Book #6)
ALL FOR ME (Book #7)
ALL IN (Book #8)

CORA SHIELDS MYSTERY SERIES
UNDONE (Book #1)
UNWANTED (Book #2)
UNHINGED (Book #3)
UNSAID (Book #4)
UNGLUED (Book #5)
UNSTABLE (Book #6)
UNKNOWN (Book #7)
UNAWARE (Book #8)

MAY MOORE SUSPENSE THRILLER
NEVER RUN (Book #1)

NEVER TELL (Book #2)
NEVER LIVE (Book #3)
NEVER HIDE (Book #4)
NEVER FORGIVE (Book #5)
NEVER AGAIN (Book #6)
NEVER LOOK BACK (Book #7)
NEVER FORGET (Book #8)
NEVER LET GO (Book #9)
NEVER PRETEND (Book #10)
NEVER HESITATE (Book #11)

PAIGE KING MYSTERY SERIES
THE GIRL HE PINED (Book #1)
THE GIRL HE CHOSE (Book #2)
THE GIRL HE TOOK (Book #3)
THE GIRL HE WISHED (Book #4)
THE GIRL HE CROWNED (Book #5)
THE GIRL HE WATCHED (Book #6)
THE GIRL HE WANTED (Book #7)
THE GIRL HE CLAIMED (Book #8)

VALERIE LAW MYSTERY SERIES
NO MERCY (Book #1)
NO PITY (Book #2)
NO FEAR (Book #3)
NO SLEEP (Book #4)
NO QUARTER (Book #5)
NO CHANCE (Book #6)
NO REFUGE (Book #7)
NO GRACE (Book #8)
NO ESCAPE (Book #9)

RACHEL GIFT MYSTERY SERIES
HER LAST WISH (Book #1)
HER LAST CHANCE (Book #2)
HER LAST HOPE (Book #3)
HER LAST FEAR (Book #4)
HER LAST CHOICE (Book #5)
HER LAST BREATH (Book #6)
HER LAST MISTAKE (Book #7)

HER LAST DESIRE (Book #8)
HER LAST REGRET (Book #9)
HER LAST HOUR (Book #10)
HER LAST SHOT (Book #11)
HER LAST PRAYER (Book #12)
HER LAST LIE (Book #13)

AVA GOLD MYSTERY SERIES
CITY OF PREY (Book #1)
CITY OF FEAR (Book #2)
CITY OF BONES (Book #3)
CITY OF GHOSTS (Book #4)
CITY OF DEATH (Book #5)
CITY OF VICE (Book #6)

A YEAR IN EUROPE
A MURDER IN PARIS (Book #1)
DEATH IN FLORENCE (Book #2)
VENGEANCE IN VIENNA (Book #3)
A FATALITY IN SPAIN (Book #4)

ELLA DARK FBI SUSPENSE THRILLER
GIRL, ALONE (Book #1)
GIRL, TAKEN (Book #2)
GIRL, HUNTED (Book #3)
GIRL, SILENCED (Book #4)
GIRL, VANISHED (Book 5)
GIRL ERASED (Book #6)
GIRL, FORSAKEN (Book #7)
GIRL, TRAPPED (Book #8)
GIRL, EXPENDABLE (Book #9)
GIRL, ESCAPED (Book #10)
GIRL, HIS (Book #11)
GIRL, LURED (Book #12)
GIRL, MISSING (Book #13)
GIRL, UNKNOWN (Book #14)
GIRL, DECEIVED (Book #15)
GIRL, FORLORN (Book #16)
GIRL, REMADE (Book #17)
GIRL, BETRAYED (Book #18)

GIRL, BOUND (Book #19)
GIRL, REFORMED (Book #20)
GIRL, REBORN (Book #21)

LAURA FROST FBI SUSPENSE THRILLER
ALREADY GONE (Book #1)
ALREADY SEEN (Book #2)
ALREADY TRAPPED (Book #3)
ALREADY MISSING (Book #4)
ALREADY DEAD (Book #5)
ALREADY TAKEN (Book #6)
ALREADY CHOSEN (Book #7)
ALREADY LOST (Book #8)
ALREADY HIS (Book #9)
ALREADY LURED (Book #10)
ALREADY COLD (Book #11)

EUROPEAN VOYAGE COZY MYSTERY SERIES
MURDER (AND BAKLAVA) (Book #1)
DEATH (AND APPLE STRUDEL) (Book #2)
CRIME (AND LAGER) (Book #3)
MISFORTUNE (AND GOUDA) (Book #4)
CALAMITY (AND A DANISH) (Book #5)
MAYHEM (AND HERRING) (Book #6)

ADELE SHARP MYSTERY SERIES
LEFT TO DIE (Book #1)
LEFT TO RUN (Book #2)
LEFT TO HIDE (Book #3)
LEFT TO KILL (Book #4)
LEFT TO MURDER (Book #5)
LEFT TO ENVY (Book #6)
LEFT TO LAPSE (Book #7)
LEFT TO VANISH (Book #8)
LEFT TO HUNT (Book #9)
LEFT TO FEAR (Book #10)
LEFT TO PREY (Book #11)
LEFT TO LURE (Book #12)
LEFT TO CRAVE (Book #13)
LEFT TO LOATHE (Book #14)

LEFT TO HARM (Book #15)
LEFT TO RUIN (Book #16)

THE AU PAIR SERIES
ALMOST GONE (Book#1)
ALMOST LOST (Book #2)
ALMOST DEAD (Book #3)

ZOE PRIME MYSTERY SERIES
FACE OF DEATH (Book#1)
FACE OF MURDER (Book #2)
FACE OF FEAR (Book #3)
FACE OF MADNESS (Book #4)
FACE OF FURY (Book #5)
FACE OF DARKNESS (Book #6)

A JESSIE HUNT PSYCHOLOGICAL SUSPENSE SERIES
THE PERFECT WIFE (Book #1)
THE PERFECT BLOCK (Book #2)
THE PERFECT HOUSE (Book #3)
THE PERFECT SMILE (Book #4)
THE PERFECT LIE (Book #5)
THE PERFECT LOOK (Book #6)
THE PERFECT AFFAIR (Book #7)
THE PERFECT ALIBI (Book #8)
THE PERFECT NEIGHBOR (Book #9)
THE PERFECT DISGUISE (Book #10)
THE PERFECT SECRET (Book #11)
THE PERFECT FAÇADE (Book #12)
THE PERFECT IMPRESSION (Book #13)
THE PERFECT DECEIT (Book #14)
THE PERFECT MISTRESS (Book #15)
THE PERFECT IMAGE (Book #16)
THE PERFECT VEIL (Book #17)
THE PERFECT INDISCRETION (Book #18)
THE PERFECT RUMOR (Book #19)
THE PERFECT COUPLE (Book #20)
THE PERFECT MURDER (Book #21)
THE PERFECT HUSBAND (Book #22)
THE PERFECT SCANDAL (Book #23)

THE PERFECT MASK (Book #24)
THE PERFECT RUSE (Book #25)
THE PERFECT VENEER (Book #26)
THE PERFECT PEOPLE (Book #27)
THE PERFECT WITNESS (Book #28)
THE PERFECT APPEARANCE (Book #29)
THE PERFECT TRAP (Book #30)
THE PERFECT EXPRESSION (Book #31)
THE PERFECT ACCOMPLICE (Book #32)
THE PERFECT SHOW (Book #33)
THE PERFECT POISE (Book #34)
THE PERFECT CROWD (Book #35)

CHLOE FINE PSYCHOLOGICAL SUSPENSE SERIES
NEXT DOOR (Book #1)
A NEIGHBOR'S LIE (Book #2)
CUL DE SAC (Book #3)
SILENT NEIGHBOR (Book #4)
HOMECOMING (Book #5)
TINTED WINDOWS (Book #6)

KATE WISE MYSTERY SERIES
IF SHE KNEW (Book #1)
IF SHE SAW (Book #2)
IF SHE RAN (Book #3)
IF SHE HID (Book #4)
IF SHE FLED (Book #5)
IF SHE FEARED (Book #6)
IF SHE HEARD (Book #7)

THE MAKING OF RILEY PAIGE SERIES
WATCHING (Book #1)
WAITING (Book #2)
LURING (Book #3)
TAKING (Book #4)
STALKING (Book #5)
KILLING (Book #6)

RILEY PAIGE MYSTERY SERIES
ONCE GONE (Book #1)

ONCE TAKEN (Book #2)
ONCE CRAVED (Book #3)
ONCE LURED (Book #4)
ONCE HUNTED (Book #5)
ONCE PINED (Book #6)
ONCE FORSAKEN (Book #7)
ONCE COLD (Book #8)
ONCE STALKED (Book #9)
ONCE LOST (Book #10)
ONCE BURIED (Book #11)
ONCE BOUND (Book #12)
ONCE TRAPPED (Book #13)
ONCE DORMANT (Book #14)
ONCE SHUNNED (Book #15)
ONCE MISSED (Book #16)
ONCE CHOSEN (Book #17)

MACKENZIE WHITE MYSTERY SERIES
BEFORE HE KILLS (Book #1)
BEFORE HE SEES (Book #2)
BEFORE HE COVETS (Book #3)
BEFORE HE TAKES (Book #4)
BEFORE HE NEEDS (Book #5)
BEFORE HE FEELS (Book #6)
BEFORE HE SINS (Book #7)
BEFORE HE HUNTS (Book #8)
BEFORE HE PREYS (Book #9)
BEFORE HE LONGS (Book #10)
BEFORE HE LAPSES (Book #11)
BEFORE HE ENVIES (Book #12)
BEFORE HE STALKS (Book #13)
BEFORE HE HARMS (Book #14)

AVERY BLACK MYSTERY SERIES
CAUSE TO KILL (Book #1)
CAUSE TO RUN (Book #2)
CAUSE TO HIDE (Book #3)
CAUSE TO FEAR (Book #4)
CAUSE TO SAVE (Book #5)
CAUSE TO DREAD (Book #6)

KERI LOCKE MYSTERY SERIES
A TRACE OF DEATH (Book #1)
A TRACE OF MURDER (Book #2)
A TRACE OF VICE (Book #3)
A TRACE OF CRIME (Book #4)
A TRACE OF HOPE (Book #5)

Made in the USA
Middletown, DE
25 February 2024